More Praise for IRA BERKOWITZ:

"A sharp, clean, and precise piece of crime writing, *Old Flame* is not to be missed. Ira Berkowitz drops you into Hell's Kitchen and leaves you wanting for more."

—**Michael Harvey,** author of *The Chicago Way* and co-creator of *Cold Case Files*

"In Hell's Kitchen, *Old Flame* burns white hot. If gritty New York streets and rough-and-tumble detectives turn you on, read this book."

—**Reed Farrel Coleman,** Shamus and Anthony Award–winning author of *Soul Patch*

"Ira Berkowitz's world-weary ex-cop is right out of Hammett and Chandler. Cynical, wisecracking, and full of snappy dialog, *Old Flame* is a **valentine to hardboiled fiction fans** and a great introduction to the genre for anyone looking for a good story and a reluctant hero. **If Berkowitz doesn't write more books about Steeg, I may send a goon to sock him in the kisser.**"

—**Chelsea Cain,** *New York Times* bestselling author of *Heartsick*

"*Old Flame* is **a mean, lean piece of noir** full of tough talk, hard men, and harder women. It's a **tense walk down a dark alley, a heart-pounding chase on the gritty streets of New York that ends with a punch in the jaw.**"

—**Lisa Unger,** *New York Times* bestselling author of *Beautiful Lies* and *Black Out*

OLD FLAME

OLD FLAME

A JACKSON STEEG NOVEL

IRA BERKOWITZ

 THREE RIVERS PRESS • NEW YORK

Copyright © 2008 by Ira Berkowitz

Published in the United States by Three Rivers Press, an imprint of the Crown Publishing Group, a division of Random House, Inc., New York.
www.crownpublishing.com

Three Rivers Press and the Tugboat design are registered trademarks of Random House, Inc.

Library of Congress Cataloging-in-Publication Data
Berkowitz, Ira.
Old flame: a Jackson Steeg novel / Ira Berkowitz.—1st ed.
    1. Ex–police officers—New York (State)—New York—Fiction.   2. Friends—
Fiction.   3. Gangsters—Fiction.   4. New York (N.Y.)—Fiction.   I. Title.
PS3602.E7573O43 2008
813'.6—dc22   2008005177

ISBN 978-0-307-40862-4

Printed in the United States of America

Design by Helene Berinsky

10 9 8 7 6 5 4 3 2 1

First Edition

For Danny, Robin, David, Allison, and Michael.

With love.

All through dinner she sensed something was wrong.

The group at the next table was partying hard, knocking back drinks and growing more raucous as the evening wore on. But she knew that wasn't it. It was over between them, and the only thing left was to speak the words.

The possibility had been brewing for some time. During the last few months, he had become more distracted. Edgier. The easy smile gone.

A couple sitting at a nearby banquette held hands and spoke low to each other. And she envied them. If this was the end, he had picked the perfect place. Formal. Public. A place where scenes were frowned on. Not that she would have made a scene. It wasn't her style. And he should have known that. But if it was over, it was time for the charade to end. She had to know. Now.

She broke the uncomfortable silence.

"This has gone on long enough," she said. "We have to talk about it. Tell me what's wrong."

He looked past her, staring off into the distance.

"Nothing."

A shriek of laughter came from the next table, and she reached down for her pocketbook.

"Let's change tables," she said.

He put a restraining hand on hers.

"No," he said. "They're not bothering me."

"Then what is, damn it?"

He waited several moments, deciding whether to confide in her, wondering how she would react.

"It started a few months ago with the phone calls," he finally said.

It wasn't the answer she expected.

"What phone calls?"

"To my cell phone. Long silences, and then a hang-up. Eight to ten a day. Sometimes more. Some at work. Some early in the evening. Some later. It gave me the creeps."

Her relief turned to anger.

"Why didn't you tell me? Isn't that what people who care about each other do?"

"I didn't want to worry you."

The simple honesty of his answer was enough to mollify her.

"I called the telephone company," he said. "They said the calls came from a prepaid cell phone. A disposable. There was nothing they could do. I changed the number. The calls continued. Always from a different number.

"Suddenly," he continued, "the pattern changed. There was a voice at the other end."

"What did it say?"

" 'Get out!' "

"That's it? 'Get out'? Of where?"

"I don't know. There's more, though."

He reached into his pocket, pulled out a sheet of paper, and handed it to her.

While she read, he gazed out the window at the white ribbon of traffic stretching as far as he could see. Just beyond was the black ribbon of the Hudson. The image curled his lips into a bitter smile. Two ribbons. One black. One white. Light and dark. Good and evil. The way of the world.

She put down the paper.

"This is awful," she said.

"It is."

A waiter appeared at the next table with a giant cupcake. A sparkler was stuck in the middle. Five people serenaded the sixth—a woman in her midtwenties—with a spirited version of "Happy Birthday" and toasted her with flutes of champagne. Her cheeks were flushed with excitement.

"Have you shown this to the police?" she said.

He continued to stare out the window, and the bitter smile reappeared. "Are you kidding?"

"I'm frightened," she said. "Whoever sent this means business. For Godsakes, we've got to—"

He cut her off. "It's meant for me, not you."

"So that makes it all right?"

"I won't let anything happen to you."

She reached over and took his hand. The color was gone from her cheeks.

"Who's doing this?" she said.

"I have my suspicions."

She waited for him to elaborate.

Instead, he signaled for the bill.

As the waiter approached, the birthday girl thrust a camera into his hand and asked him to take pictures. When he had snapped a few, she gave the camera to her friend and draped her body around the red-faced waiter. More photos.

"The only thing I believe is that I want to get the hell out of here," he said. He peeled three one-hundred-dollar bills from a roll and threw them on the table.

Outside, traffic on West Street slowed as the occupants of the vehicles watched a Coast Guard cutter, its running lights ablaze, head upriver.

It was almost midnight, and the street was empty of pedestrians.

She took his arm and cuddled up close as they walked to his car. "I want to talk about this some more," she said. "We just can't do nothing."

"I'm done talking. I'll handle it."

They rounded the corner, and he stopped and turned around for one more look at the river.

"It's the damnedest thing," he said.

"What is?"

"Look at the water. See how those lights just dance on its surface, like white fire on black fire."

And then his world exploded.

J eanmarie Doyle, my ex-mother-in-law, loathed me in a biblical way, had poisoned my marriage, and now sat at my kitchen table smiling sweetly, coiled to strike again.

In the years since Ginny divorced me, Jeanmarie's black hair had turned white, her body had thickened, and deep lines crosshatched her cheeks. But if you looked closely, the same feral madness still bubbled in her eyes.

For the better part of a half hour she sipped coffee from an NYPD mug with a crack in its handle and rattled on about people I didn't remember and deaths I didn't mourn. Even though the snakes in my head screamed that she was about to screw up my life, I didn't interrupt. Jeanmarie got to things in her own time.

After the second refill, the well of small talk had run dry, and Jeanmarie got down to business.

"Steeg," she said, "I need your help."

My mother, Norah, used to say that the fairies give each of us a measure of cheek at birth. And as the years pile up on each other, all we're left with is humility. It was fair to say

Jeanmarie's measure had a long way to go before the larder was empty.

The sheer chutzpah of the woman was astounding.

The snakes had had enough. I got up from the table, walked to the door, and held it open.

"Have a nice day, Jeanmarie."

"It's not for me I'm asking, it's for Ginny."

That got my attention.

"Ginny and her husband are getting death threats," she said. "I'm not surprised. It was a match I didn't approve of."

She wrinkled her nose and glanced out the window at a pale and listless day.

"But she's my child," Jeanmarie continued, "and I only want for her happiness."

I had heard Ginny had married a fireman, a Lower East Side guy named Gerhardt. But, as I recall, there wasn't much Jeanmarie, or her husband, Ollie, did approve of, so I didn't pursue it.

I walked back to the kitchen.

"Did she go to the police?" I asked.

She looked at me as if I were an idiot child.

Jeanmarie Doyle was about three things: family, the Church, and hatred for the British avocation of fucking the Irish over every chance they got. Strongbow, Cromwell, the plantations, the Rising, the Troubles weren't history. They were festering, real-time events that she took with tea at night and with oatmeal in the morning. She even kept a kitchen canister for loose change and the spare dollar, periodically collected by the Hell's Kitchen IRA man.

But above all, Jeanmarie hated and distrusted the police, a fact that had never boded well for my relationship with her daughter. When Ginny announced that she planned to marry a cop—me—it caused a shit storm of epic proportions. Cops, especially if they were Irish, were the enemy. Jeanmarie had fought our marriage every step of the way, but Ginny was resolute. So Jeanmarie bit her lip and pasted on a smile, but she never got past it.

Yet here she was, in my kitchen.

"I didn't raise my child to go to the cops for justice," she said.

"I'm a cop and you're here," I said.

A little smile, faintly cruel, I thought, played on her lips, and I knew exactly what she was thinking. The nine that tore through my chest courtesy of Frankie One-Eye, a meth-stoked pimp, had been God's punishment for the way I earned my living. A kind of balancing of the scales.

"Not anymore," she said.

"Fair point."

Neither of us spoke for a few minutes as the obvious question hung uncomfortably in the air. In the distance, a ship's horn sounded. Loud. Not from a tug. Something much bigger.

"Why are *you* here instead of Ginny?"

She splayed her fingers on the table and gazed at them.

"It wouldn't be seemly," she said.

"Seemly?"

"Aye. You being her ex and all."

Suddenly, I was back in Lace Curtain Hell with its bullshit traditions and circumscriptions. I could have pointed out that her son, Liam, a petty thief with a lengthy rap sheet, hardly fit the description of seemly. Neither did her daughter Colleen, a stone drunk who hooked whenever the unemployment insurance ran out. And then there was her husband, Ollie, who by reason of laziness, inadequacy, or happenstance occupied a premier spot on the wrong side of society's bell curve.

"Does Ginny know you're here?"

Jeanmarie shook her head.

"All I want is to help my little girl." She leaned forward and gripped my hands. "No matter what has gone on before, you're still family. And that counts for something." Her grip tightened and her voice grew cold. "I want you to find the bastards and kill them."

The real Jeanmarie had finally made an appearance. Her mad eyes fastened on mine and refused to let go.

The muscles in my neck bunched up.

When I was on the job, I spent my time awash in the truly terrible things people were capable of. Ever since the shooting, I'd tried to balance things a bit by hitting the museums and galleries and whatever else piqued my interest. Jeanmarie sparked a memory of an exhibition of Spanish painting I'd seen at the Guggenheim a few weeks ago. There was one work that kept pulling me back. The background was a dense black. In the foreground a gray-robed monk held a saint's skull. And beneath the cowl, wreathed in shadows, the mere suggestion of a face. The scene struck me as a place of preternatural madness, somewhere on the doorstep of hell. I still wondered about the effect the painting had on me. The only thing I could come up with is that the artist and I saw the same demons, shared the same snakes. Wallowed in their muck.

And now I was in danger of getting lost in the muck again. But this time it was Jeanmarie's head. A place of dark, swirling Celtic mists, of vendetta and retribution, a place of blood for blood.

I owed her nothing. The local cops could handle it, and

Ginny was smart enough to bring them in when things started going downhill. Besides, whatever Jeanmarie said about "family," thanks to my love affair with Johnnie Black, I didn't even remember large chunks of my marriage—except for the sex. And that was very good. Funny how some things stand out, while others kind of recede into the fog.

I was about to tell Jeanmarie to piss off when the phone rang.

"Gotta talk to Jeanmarie," Ollie said, the words colliding into each other.

I handed her the phone. "It's your husband."

"Ollie?" she said.

Other than a slight tightening around her eyes, Jeanmarie's face showed nothing. "Where?" she whispered into the receiver. "Tell her I'm on my way."

She handed me the phone. "It's happened," she said. "They murdered Ginny's husband."

An old Irish beat cop I once knew passed on some pretty good advice: Steer clear of painted women, men who could make the ace of spades leap out of a deck of cards and croon "Danny Boy," and the irretrievably insane. I was about to violate rule number three.

Jeanmarie gave me the location of the crime scene—the West Village, on the river, in the Meatpacking District.

Like Hell's Kitchen, the Meatpacking District is in transition. Translation: It's another old-line neighborhood that's become a gleam in the eye of real-estate developers hell-bent on taking the fun out of the city.

I still wasn't sure that this had anything to do with me. The last time I got tangled up with family, it turned into a rat's nest. But the juxtaposition of events—Jeanmarie's visit coinciding with the murder of Ginny's husband—had all the makings of a cosmic invitation. And, for all of my bullshit to the contrary, I was curious, completely ignoring what curiosity did to the cat.

The clouds had thickened, and the air had the coppery

smell of rain, but I was betting against. The District was two miles south of Hell's Kitchen, and I decided to walk. I needed the exercise. At Forty-second Street I lost the bet. The rain started as a shpritz, but it was enough to send the crowd lining up to buy tickets at the Circle Line Cruise depot running for cover. I pulled my collar up and waited for the light to change.

"Fuckin' tourists! They're killin' this city."

That pithy observation came from a short guy with a shaved head who appeared to be nine months pregnant.

"Take our jobs and send the money back to wherever the fuck they come from. Probably don't even support our troops. Am I right, or what?" he said.

For some reason, I seem to attract the psychos. First, Jean-marie, and now this joker. The day hadn't even started and I was worn out. "Take a hike," I said.

He edged away.

The light changed.

I kept going, crossing the street to walk along the river. The rain came down harder, making dull pocking sounds as it hit the water. Across from the Javits Center a burnout home-less guy wearing every article of clothing he owned searched the sidewalk for cigarette butts. The rain cut down on his chances.

In twenty minutes I was at the southern edge of Chelsea. Several blocks down I saw the crime scene. It was hard to miss. Two patrol cars, one unmarked, and the coroner's wagon clogged Thirteenth Street. As I got closer, I noticed that all the activity appeared to be focused on an alley adjacent to Été, a glossy new restaurant specializing in Thai-French fusion.

I couldn't even imagine what that meant. A sprinkling of the local gentry—trannies, street hustlers, truckers, and workmen—stood at the head of the alley looking at the coroner's folks bagging the body.

The uniforms had lost interest, and the crime-scene folks were packing up their bags, but Detective Pete Toal lingered behind, taking notes. I didn't recognize his partner, a tall, young guy with thinning blond hair and the beginnings of a potbelly.

"Hey, Pete," I called. "Still at it, huh?"

"Steeg, how're you doing?" he said. "Come on in and see what real cops do for a living."

I ducked under the tape.

The alley was long and narrow, and thick with the smell of rotting food. Some manic street artist had gone off his meds and slathered the walls with hollow-eyed creatures floating amid swirls and blotches of red and black paint. A vision of the hell he saw in his head. A dumpster with chipped green paint stood against the far wall. The body bag lay in a puddle just in front.

Pete slipped his notepad into his jacket pocket and held out his hand. "Been too long, man," he said, pulling me in for a hug. "I know you're off the job, but still. You don't call, you don't write, don't you love me anymore?"

Pete and I had gone through the Academy together and discovered that we shared a taste for booze, and a friendship was born. The difference was that he could put away gallons of the stuff and it never got in the way. With me, it *was* the way.

"You know how it goes," I said. "Stuff happens. Things change."

He nodded. "They do indeed. It was a good thing you did, blowing that guy off the planet. One less piece of shit on the streets."

I nodded.

"Last I heard, you were with the Anti-Terrorism Task Force," I said. "When did you move to Homicide?"

"About a year ago. Talk about a Chinese fire drill. In Anti-Terrorism all the bosses are up your ass 24/7, then you got four or five federal law enforcement agencies tripping over themselves."

"Sounds like a treat."

"Tell me about it. And to top it all off, you got a bunch of truly scary hard cases, snake-eaters, who look like they can take down a small country with a Swiss Army knife. And when you throw in the fucking politicians all elbowing for face time with the press, it's, shall we say, tension-filled. So I said, Fuck it, and moved into something a little less harrowing."

"Who's your partner?"

"Arne Jensen. Very earnest young man. All about truth, justice, and the American way. Makes my hemorrhoids throb. Plus, he wants to be called Swede."

"Swede. Catchy."

" 'Course, no one does it. 'Suck Up' works just fine."

"Seems kind of young for a shot at the brass ring," I said. "It took me years before I got my gold badge."

"Excellent deduction, Sherlock. The hump's connected somehow. Been on the job three years, and he gets to work with the big, swinging homicide dicks. For all I know, the commissioner is his rabbi." He shrugged. "Who gives a shit? In a couple of years I'll have my pension. I've got a security job lined up. No muss, no fuss, and home at six in one piece." He squinted at me through the raindrops. "So, what're you doing here?"

"Your vic might be my ex-wife's husband. Guy named Gerhardt."

"You got the wrong crime scene, pally. According to his ID, my stiff is Tony Ferris."

"How could that be?"

"Maybe you got bad information. You say Ginny married this guy?"

"Yeah."

"Well, you're in for another shocker."

Toal took my arm and walked me over to the body bag. He knelt and pulled the zipper down.

The surprises just kept on coming.

Tony Ferris was black.

My head was buzzing with exes.

My ex-mother-in-law shows up to tell me that my ex-wife and her husband are getting death threats. The husband winds up dead, so someone followed through. I thought the stiff was Husband Number Two. Turns out he was Husband Number Three. Lucky for Husband Number Two, but still very confusing. Since confusion usually makes me hungry, I headed over to Feeney's for a late breakfast and a little quiet to sort things out. Except for the two guys sitting at either end of the bar nursing their morning whiskey, the place was empty.

Feeney's is a hole-in-the-wall Hell's Kitchen saloon dating back to Prohibition. Now it serves as an oasis for barely socialized individuals who take their drinking seriously and find comfort in doing it alone.

I parked myself in a booth and pondered the problem, especially its very large wrinkle. Why didn't Jeanmarie mention that Ferris was black? Could it be that Ferris's race was something she had come to terms with, and therefore it was unimportant?

Nah! Not to Jeanmarie. In her world even Black Irish didn't make the cut. Jeanmarie was an equal opportunity hater, as was her husband, Ollie, a bottom-of-the-barrel guy who lived his entire life locked in a snow globe of the eternally pissed-off. And Ferris wasn't married to just any white woman. Ginny was the daughter of Jeanmarie and Ollie, a fact not easily dismissed.

The only other fact I had was that Ferris had been threatened about something and didn't take it seriously. His killer obviously did.

But threatened about what?

It was at that moment that I knew I had slipped from mild curiosity to something bordering on interest. To make matters worse, I had fallen into the trap of putting together a list of suspects. The realization didn't make me happy. For the past year my days had passed peacefully. I had pretty much rehabbed from my bullet wound, and the only thing that was off the table was heavy lifting and running the marathon. And I had the pension. Not much, but enough. Life was reasonably good.

And I was about to screw it up again.

"Since when did I become your fucking answering service?"

I looked up to find Nick D'Amico, the proprietor of the joint, looming over me. Nick was a made guy who'd gone his own way after Joe Colombo bought it at an Italian-American Civil Rights League rally and his Family fell into turmoil. Ever since, Nick worked for my brother, Dave. Nick was as much an anachronism as his saloon. To outsiders, Nick was a happy-go-lucky muffin who closed the place down to his regular customers on Christmas Eve and threw a party for the neighborhood homeless. They never saw the stone killer who would turn you into origami over a slight.

"I'd be happy to take my business elsewhere," I said.

"What business? You don't drink no more, and what you eat here ain't gonna get me that condo on Park Avenue anytime soon."

"Look at the bright side. You won't have all those people to tip at Christmas."

He shrugged his agreement. "That condo on Park was almost a possibility. I got an offer for the building."

I wasn't surprised. Hell's Kitchen was hot. Most of the buildings wore scaffolding like leis. And perfectly formed thirty-somethings, all decked out in "vintage" sneakers and shirts with little polo players on the pockets, prowled the streets sizing up the area, using words like *charming* and *quaint*.

"And?"

"Told them to stick it up their ass."

Worked for me.

"Who called?" I said.

"Allie, and your old buddy Danny Reno. She was back from San Francisco and heading into a meeting."

"And Reno?"

"Who gives a shit? Didn't sound too happy, though."

One out of two wasn't bad.

Allie was Allison Lebow, the love of my life and reigning creative director at Bellknap & Hoskins, an advertising agency that had recently set up shop on Tenth and Fifty-second.

We met purely by chance at a particularly nasty deli near her office. She was grilling the counterman, a bearded and turbaned Sikh, on whether the seeds on her bagel were poppy or the desiccated exoskeletons of tiny insects. Poppy, he assured her. She wasn't buying it, and things were getting ugly. Her mood ring had turned from a pretty blue color to angry black. I stepped in. A quick nibble was all it took. Bug casings, for sure. We've been together ever since.

"She's good for you. I see it."

"I agree."

"You're not such a fucking mood-buster no more."

"Is there a compliment in there?"

"Take it for what it is," he said. "You did a good thing taking Frankie off the map. Look, we all do what we have to do to earn, but it was never business with that twisted, shit-brained fuck. So I figured maybe you'd be a little happy. But no, you turned into a pissy mope. Until you met Allie."

When a whore's earning power had slipped, Frankie One-Eye, a greasy-looking lowlife with bad skin and a milky eye, was her final stop in the pimp marketplace. Frankie bought these poor crack zombies at a deep discount and put them to work in sex shows he ran in the backs of semis in the Meatpacking District. Their time with Frankie was brief. When they no longer amused his equally lowlife customers, or him, they wound up dead, but we were never able to nail him. Frankie became my personal White Whale when he turned a young girl in his employ—a sad-eyed, tiny little thing I kind of looked out for—into a Hudson River floater. Once again, Frankie proved to be the Teflon pimp, but I saw it as a minor inconvenience. Getting into his oatmeal became my reason for being. It didn't take long for him to snap, and when he did, I took the top of his head off. But not before he almost returned the favor by putting a nine in my chest. Given my unorthodox handling of the situation, the folks at One Police Plaza did a quick investigation, decided to call it a righteous shooting, and put the lid on. Tight. But they figured that it would be better for everyone if my recuperation lasted forever. In exchange for my gold shield they gave me a medal and a disability pension.

Yeah, popping Frankie was a very good thing, but he turned out to be the gift that just keeps on giving; the one monster in my pantheon of night demons that set all the others free to frolic inside my head. At least until Allie came along. When she was with me, the monsters weren't.

"Love gives the heart ease, and she keeps the snakes in my head from rioting," I told Nick.

Nick slipped into the booth and sat opposite me. His powder blue Banlon shirt fit him like a sausage casing. "That may be," he said, "but today you don't look too happy."

"Ginny's husband got iced."

"Who gives a shit? The day she left you she ceased to exist. I don't give a fuck what happens to her or her husband, and neither should you."

Nick had known me ever since I was a kid, and loyalty was high up on the very short list of things he cared about.

"Her mother asked me to look into it."

"The Dragon Lady? You gotta be kidding! When you were married to her daughter, fucking Jeanmarie wouldn't cross the street to piss on you if you were on fire." He reached over and rapped his knuckles on my forehead. "What's going on in there? The slug took out part of your lung, not your brain."

"I didn't say I'd do it. I'm just thinking about it."

"I know you better. Walk away. No, make that *run away*. And here's something else: I know you and Ginny were married and all, but the apple don't fall far from the tree."

I should have listened.

I called Pete Toal and got Ginny's address.

According to the Hertz map, Seaside was nestled in the middle of Long Island, smack dab in the crotch of the Twin Forks and, in a bit of developer tomfoolery, nowhere near the sea.

The combination of a dogged, slanting rain and a salmon run of crosstown traffic nearly gave me second thoughts. The Long Island Expressway was more of the same. Construction had backed traffic up for miles, but once I got past exit 40, I was speeding along at a blurring twenty miles an hour. After another ten exits, stands of tall trees just coming into bud flanked the highway, obscuring the sprawling exurbia of Civilserviceville.

Once, city workers actually lived in the city. Now, most have pushed the envelope to the outer reaches of the New York metro area. The commute is a daily stick in the eye, but a city job, even at the top of the pay scale, barely covers the rent on a shitty two-bedroom in an equally shitty neighborhood teeming with crime beggaring description. Out here in Civilserviceville, things are different. Home ownership is a God-given right, kids actually learn useful things in schools, no one kills them for their iPods, and the skies are not cloudy all day.

A definite no-brainer.

Three plus hours later I saw the sign for Seaside. The good news was, the rain had stopped. The bad news was, I was in a place that looked remarkably like Kansas.

A jillion years ago, glaciers had flattened Long Island, and it never recovered from the trauma. As far as the eye could see, miles of tract houses interrupted only by shopping centers and office parks—an oxymoron of titanic proportions—marched to the horizon.

Ginny's house was a tract ranch fronted by a tidy, postage-stamp lawn and leafy foundation plantings, sitting cheek by jowl with other ranches with tidy patches of grass and leafy foundation plantings. Everything was laid out with geometric precision. The word *soulless* popped into my mind. It was hard imagining Ginny living in a place like this. It was hard imagining *anyone* living in a place like this.

Ginny and I were neighborhood kids who married, grew up, and, after a few years, divorced. Our marriage began in high teenage wattage and unraveled stitch by stitch. For a while I blamed the breakup on my drinking, convinced myself that though my life was spiraling into the toilet, it was a good thing she wasn't willing to go along for the ride. But that wasn't it.

Were we in love? That was, and I guess still is, an open question. But when you cut right through it, we were never a fit. Never one bone. Never one skin.

Another Hell's Kitchen Station of the Cross.

We had met at the Church of the Most Precious Blood Confraternity Dance. I was seventeen; she was a year younger and a stunner. And for some unfathomable reason totally smitten with me. A shock, since adolescence wasn't my best moment. I could only ascribe my good fortune to pheromones.

We began dating and quickly became what was known in the neighborhood as an "item." When I turned eighteen, I embarked on the first leg of your basic Hell's Kitchen life journey. I enlisted in the Marine Corps. When my tour in Desert Storm was up, I came home.

Instead of getting a job and settling in for the long haul, I crossed everyone up and enrolled in City College, and Ginny and I picked up where we left off. Two years later we married, and it was time to earn a living. I bid academia a reluctant good-bye and went on the force. Given the other choices—blue-collar work, or a job strong-arming people for my brother, Dave—it was a reasonable alternative. Do twenty years on the job, have a couple of kids, buy a summer cottage in the Poconos, cash the tax-free pension check, and if things got tight, there was always a security-guard job out there on the horizon. A pleasant life trajectory.

But there was a snake in the Garden. The Marines had taken me out of the Kitchen and into the world. And I liked what I saw.

When my tour was up, the Kitchen seemed a lot less interesting, and I wanted out. Ginny didn't. We were headed in different directions. In the end, she was the one who left. I thought I would never see her again. Over was over. Besides, I'd had Johnnie B for company.

Funny how things turn out.

I pulled into her driveway and parked alongside a silver SUV.

I got out of the car and went to the door. It swung open before I had a chance to knock.

"Hi, Jake," she said.

Two words.

That's all it took.

A jarring intimacy, the special kind of knowing that only comes from someone who has read your soul and knows all of your sins.

Time had sharpened the once soft lines of her face. Her honey blond hair—auburn, when she served me with divorce papers—was tied tightly in a ponytail, making the angles even sharper. She wore a black velvet warm-up suit that was never intended to see a droplet of sweat, and pink step-in sneakers. A cute little hood sagged between her shoulder blades.

Hardly widow's weeds.

She threw her arms around me. I got a whiff of expensive perfume and the sharp smell of gin. It surprised me. Except for the occasional beer with dinner, Ginny wasn't a drinker. I guess grief went well with gin.

"This is a surprise," she said, stepping back and mustering a weak smile. "Long Island is way off your beat."

"It's been a long time since I've had a beat."

She threaded her arm around mine and led me into the living room.

The room was decorated in Hell's Kitchen Luxe—expensive, but gaudy. Lots of heavy, dark wood, downy cushioned sofas, acres of plush carpeting, and lampshades with crystal thingies hanging from their bottoms. I settled in on the sofa and sunk to my hips. Ginny sat down beside me.

"It's been a while," she said.

"Ten years."

"Doesn't seem like it."

"I expected Jeanmarie to answer the door," I said.

"She left a little while ago. Told me she came to see you. I wish she hadn't."

"Why's that?"

"You don't need any more crap in your life."

"That's my call, isn't it?"

"I heard about your dad. I liked Dominic."

"Everyone liked Dominic, except Dominic."

"And I heard about you. I'm so sorry."

I shrugged. "The million-dollar wound. I've got the pension and I'm alive. A fair trade. And I'm off the sauce. Amazing how different the world looks when you're upright. Tell me about you. I heard you married a fireman."

She studied her very long French-tipped nails, and a brittle smile played on her lips.

"Yeah, but it didn't last long," she said. "He had hand trouble. The psycho thought I needed disciplining every now and again."

"My turn to say I'm sorry."

She shrugged. "What is it they say? All the bad things in your life just make you stronger?"

"Something like that."

"Are you involved with anyone?"

"I am," I said.

She nodded. "It really sucks being alone, doesn't it," she said.

"Not when you're your own best friend."

She smiled. "I forgot. You never needed anyone." She paused. "Except for Dave."

"Forever bound by the ties of filial love, my brother and I continue to march in lockstep through these mean streets. Yin and Yang."

Her eyes strayed to her hands. "Light and darkness. Black and white."

"Tell me about Tony," I said.

Her fingers toyed with a silver crucifix hanging from a slender chain around her neck.

"He works in the city—works *for* the city actually, Minority Opportunities Bureau—but we met out here. He's—he was—a decent guy, and we hit it off right away."

"How long were you married?"

"Almost six years."

"How did that go down with Jeanmarie and Ollie?"

"How do you think? They barely tolerated *you*. Tony? They wouldn't let him in their house. Ollie still doesn't talk to me. Thinks I'm some sort of a race betrayer."

"Ollie was always open-minded," I said.

"You know what really frosts me?"

"What?"

"When we were kids, come Friday night, Ollie and his buddies would be cruising black bars looking to get lucky. I know because I followed them one night. And if he didn't manage to get lucky, he'd come home, all smelling of puke and whiskey, and take it out on us." Her eyes filled. "Ollie and his buddies standing on each other's shoulders don't add up to one Tony Ferris."

She was silent for a while.

Then she turned to me.

"Does it matter to you?" she said.

"Does what matter?"

"That Tony was black."

"Should it?"

"No," she said.

"Why do you think Tony was murdered?"

She reached over to the coffee table and snagged a file.

"Take a look at this," she said.

It was some of the vilest racist crap I had ever seen. Six letters, unsigned and computer printed, and filled with dire and colorful word pictures of Tony's fate if he didn't heed the warnings to pack up and go.

I closed the file.

"Take it," she said. "They're copies. I have the originals."

"Did you show this to the police?"

"Sure."

"And?"

"A lot of good it did. He's dead."

"What do you want me to do?"

"Make things right."

Make things right.

How do you make a killing right? How do you square things? The knee-jerk answer is *closure,* the magic word du jour that means different things to different people. Another notch on the DA's belt, one less thing for the cops to deal with, the next new thing for the twenty-four-hour news cycle, and a cruel promise for the victim's family.

I called Pete Toal from the road and asked if the ME's report was in.

"No," he said. "Busy day at the coroner. Stiffs have to take a number. But I don't need the ME for a reading on this one."

"How so?"

"Perp beat the shit out of him. Lot of emotion went into his work. Especially around the groin area. Nuts are the size of volleyballs. Look, I'd love to chat, but me and Swede are off on another adventure. I'll let you know when I hear something."

Crime of passion. And I'd neglected to ask Ginny where she was last night. It would keep.

My next call was to Allie. She penciled me in for a late lunch.

The drive back to the city took hours. Thousands of people made the trip every day. I wondered how they stayed sane.

We met at a little outdoor café near her office. Apparently the pitch had gone well, and six and a half hours on the red-eye hadn't dampened the high.

With straight, nut-brown hair parted in the middle, and wearing black Nike sandals and a T-shirt bearing the rhinestone-studded inscription SURROUNDED BY MORONS tucked into her jeans, Allie looked more like a hippie graduate student who had just aced her orals than a high-powered advertising mover and shaker.

"We nailed it," she said, picking at her Cobb salad. "When I hit them with the campaign, there was a room full of smiley faces."

The restaurant had very tiny tables crowded next to each other, very large plates, very tiny portions stacked very high in the middle, and a fine sprinkling of soot for seasoning. Although it was an unusually warm day, the angle of the sunlight bore traces of winter.

A young couple sitting inches from us were having an animated and highly distracting discussion about a band performing at some club. She wanted to go, he didn't. He thought they sucked. She, not so politely, said he did. It was boring. I wanted to hear about Allie's triumph.

"About an hour into it," she continued, "I thought we were dead. The account exec was doing his marketing mambo. A lot of talk about positioning and competitive thrusts, whatever the hell that means."

"Sounds salacious."

"Would that it were. At the very least, we would have had their attention." She speared a piece of lettuce. "I swear I heard light snoring."

"And then you took center stage."

She smiled. "Yes I did."

"And saved the day."

She leaned over and planted a little peck on the tip of my nose. "That too, and not a moment too soon. Then it was the research folks' turn, and once again ennui washed over the conference room like a red tide."

"You're quite the wordsmith."

She impaled another lettuce leaf and dipped the tip in the dressing. "That's why they pay me the big bucks."

"Did you reignite their interest by showing them your discreetly positioned butterfly tattoo? It certainly helped clinch the deal with me."

"I would have if I thought it would help."

"Hussy," I said.

"No, *adwoman*," she shot back. An eyebrow rose fetchingly, and just the shadow of a smile crossed her lips. "I might arrange a private showing later on this evening."

"Have you no shame?"

"Nope."

"Another reason why I'm attracted to you. But the problem is, I'm doing homework with DeeDee and, after that, meeting Luce and Cherise at Neon. It's Cherise's birthday. It could run late."

Luce Guidry was my ex-partner, and Cherise Adams, also a cop, was her wife.

"Cherise's birthday I could understand, but homework with DeeDee?" Allie said. "She's enrolled at Stuyvesant, for Godsake. Tell me you're kidding."

DeeDee Santos was a latchkey kid who lived two flights down from me. Her father, fast of fist and slow of mind, boarded frequently at a variety of criminal holding facilities. Her mother, somewhere in the Dominican Republic, was no help. And DeeDee was left to navigate Hell's Kitchen's shoals alone. One day we connected, and we have been pals ever since. During one particularly rough spot in both our lives, she'd even temporarily moved in with me. Now she still lived with me whenever her father was incarcerated, and attended one of New York City's premier public high schools. So far, things had worked out.

"I resent the disparaging tone of your question."

"Do you! OK, what are you helping her with?"

I took a sudden interest in the haphazard way the French fries were piled on my plate and moved them around to more esthetically satisfying positions with my fork.

"She might have mentioned something about quadratic equations," I said.

"If she needed help with thug-nabbing, that I could understand, but you wouldn't know a quadratic equation from a newt."

"*Au contraire!* A newt is a tiny lizard that eats bugs. A quadratic equation is simply a second order polynomial equation in a single variable x."

She stared at me with one eyebrow arched. "You have no idea what that means, do you?"

I still hadn't gotten the fries quite where I wanted them. "Not at all," I admitted. "I looked it up on the Web."

"God help her!"

"Enough of me. Let's get back to you. When do you think you'll hear?"

She went back to her salad. Allie had an odd way of eating. Each food species was consumed separately. First the tomatoes, then the lettuce, and so on down the veggie array until it was all gone.

"They haven't made a decision yet. There are two more agencies scheduled to present. We'll know in a month, I guess."

Out of the corner of my eye I noticed a pretty woman wearing a navy blue pin-striped suit and a white silk blouse holding a cell phone to her ear. An expensive-looking attaché case sat at her feet. Tears streaming down her cheeks left faint ruts in her makeup. I tried to look away, but it was impossible. Her eyes locked on mine for the briefest of moments, flaring with resentment at my intrusion. And then, hunching her shoulders forward, she abruptly half-turned. Another mystery in a city brimming with mysteries.

I turned my attention back to Allie and told her about my suddenly burgeoning private detective business.

Allie's eyes narrowed slightly. "Your ex-wife?"

"Is there a problem?"

"Should there be?"

"Not that I can see," I said.

She smoothed the front of her T-shirt and SURROUNDED BY MORONS glittered in the afternoon light.

CHAPTER 6

Homework with DeeDee went as I had expected. It wasn't about quadratic equations, thank God. She just wanted company. We shared a sausage pizza, caught up on things, and I left around ten.

When I arrived at Neon, a sweaty gay bar on Eleventh, the lights were low and throbbing to a techno beat, and the party in full swing. I spotted Luce and Cherise, and about six of their friends, sitting at a table the size of a serving platter just off the dance floor. A birthday cake sat on the table. I worked my way through the crowd.

Luce Guidry was my ex-partner and closest friend. Born and raised in Louisiana, Luce had skin the color of chickory coffee au lait, and tastes that ran to clunky jewelry, pastel fabrics, and Cherise Adams, a cop who worked out of Brooklyn.

"Jackson," she said, with a glowing smile. "You made it."

Luce was the only person who ever used my given name.

"Wouldn't miss it for the world."

Cherise jumped up and threw her arms around me.

"You just made me ten dollars richer," she said. "Luce didn't expect you to show up until midnight, assuming you remembered. I had more faith and took the under."

"Then drinks are on you." I turned to Luce. "Happy birthday, kiddo."

"You gonna help me blow out the candles?"

"I don't know if I can handle it. So many candles, it's going to look like a forest fire."

She hauled off and landed a punch on my arm. It hit the bone and stung like hell. "Now, you be nice, Steeg," she said, throwing me a mock glare.

Cherise made a group introduction; there were nods all around. I could barely hear the names over the music. Luce pulled a chair from the next table and set it beside hers.

"You set yourself right here, Jackson, while I get you something to drink."

"Stay where you are, I'll get it."

I walked to the bar, wedged my body into a narrow gap, and tried to get the attention of the bartender, a pretty blonde with close-cropped hair and multiple lip and nose piercings, who had her hands full. Tats of graceful, twining wildflowers in soft pastels snaked around her hands and arms. Tattoos were something I never understood, but on her they seemed right.

There was a time when I would have leaped the bar to get to a drink, but now my beverage of choice was Diet Coke, and there was no urgency. Comforted by the thought, I waited.

After a few minutes, she appeared. A thin film of perspiration covered her upper lip.

She shrugged an apology. "It's one of those nights. What can I get you?"

I told her.

There was a fleeting quizzical look, and then a smiling, "Sure. Be right back."

I laid a five on the bar and turned to watch the dancers on the postage stamp–sized floor. Their moves were joyously balletic, and there wasn't five percent of body fat among them.

In a blink, everything changed.

There was the barest ripple, something a school of reef fish must sense at a predator's looming shadow. The dancers, sensing it too, slowed. The conversation at the bar dimmed, and all eyes moved to the entrance.

Three shirtless men with shaved heads, all decked out in leather vests, jeans, and thick-soled Grinders, moved to the bar. The crowd melted in their path.

This had all the makings of an interesting evening.

I glanced over at Luce's table. She and Cherise were on their feet, their hands resting lightly on the butts of their service revolvers.

I held my hand up and gestured for them to wait. Maybe this would blow over before anyone got hurt.

Nah!

All the barstools had emptied, leaving the pretty young bartender to deal with the Three Amigos alone. From the look on her face she wasn't having an easy time. I ambled over and planted myself on a stool right next to them. One of them, a huge, dull-witted-looking oaf, had a large shamrock tattooed on his scalp, the badge of Aryan Brotherhood hard cases. The other two—shorter and thinner, but equally dumb-looking—were covered in swastikas, skulls, lightning bolts, and other Nazi bullshit. All three smelled like sewage.

"How come your name tag doesn't say 'Muff Diver'?" Shamrock said to the bartender. His buddies, gibbering like monkeys, thought it was the wittiest thing they had ever heard.

"Fuck off!" she said, reddening.

"Excuse me," I said. "I believe I ordered a Diet Coke. How's about getting it for me?"

With a grateful look she retreated to the far end of the bar. I noticed that Luce and Cherise were standing there watching.

"*Diet Coke?*" Shamrock said, moving onto the stool next to mine. "The fudgepacker's drinkin' a Diet fuckin' Coke. You want a cherry with it?"

Suddenly, I felt that all-too-familiar out-of-control tingle when everything is on hair-trigger and giving a shit is off the table. A rush of superheated blood raced up from a magma chamber deep within my body. I wondered how long the cap rock would hold.

The snakes in my head grew giddy with anticipation.

"I understand you had to blow half the guys in the Brotherhood before they let you wear that shamrock."

His face darkened.

"You're talkin' about my brothers, faggot," he said.

I smiled sweetly. "Right, the guys who pimped you for cigarettes in the joint."

He drew back a fist the size of a skillet.

That was all it took. The cap rock blew, taking all reason and sanity with it and leaving me an interested observer along for the ride.

As if of its own volition, my hand grabbed a mug and drove it upward into his face. I heard the crunch of his nose flattening against his skull. Saw the bewildered panic in his eyes just before his eyes went wobbly. Watched the skinhead nearest me double over from a dropkick to the nuts and flip over backward when I kneed him in the mouth. Saw the other guy take off. *Fucking tough guys!* I thought as my blood cooled.

It was a good night's work.

Luce and Cherise ran up to me.

"Holy shit!" Luce said, surveying the wreckage. "I'd cuff them, but it appears they ain't going anywhere."

"You sure know how to party, Steeg," Cherise said.

In the distance I heard the whine of sirens. Most everyone heard it too. There was a mad dash for the door.

"I have an aversion to assholes," I said.

The pretty young bartender brought me a Diet Coke.

"Thanks," she said. "And if I ever go back to the other side I'll go looking for you."

A couple of uniforms walked in. Luce and Cherise flashed their badges. One of them looked at the two bodies on the floor, and then at Luce and Cherise.

"Whoa!" he said. "You did this?"

Luce pointed at me. "No, he did."

The uniform sized me up. "Nice," he said. "But whoever did the guy out front finished the job."

"What do you mean?"

"That's why we're here. There's a guy laying in the gutter.

Someone went to work on the poor bastard with chains. Found them in an alley. And then they stomped the shit out of him. Guy has boot prints all over what's left of his face. The security cameras should tell us more."

As it turned out, the security cameras weren't working, and there were no witnesses.

Sometimes you can't catch a break.

The next morning, Danny Reno was waiting for me at Feeney's. Nick was right. He looked like crap.

Danny and I grew up together, and just about everyone marked him as someone special, someone destined to get out of Hell's Kitchen in one piece. Unlike the rest of us, Danny was bright, polite, and could charm the nuns right out of their habits. Jack Armstrong, All-American Boy. But somewhere along the way, he went off the rails, always chasing the big score and always coming up empty.

For a while, counterfeits—pocketbooks, designer scarves, and baseball cards—were Danny's thing, and he was lousy at it. His last brainstorm was selling cut-rate tropical houseplants from the back of a van. It turned out they were diseased and went fronds-up after a day or two. A couple of disgruntled customers put him in the hospital when he told them his company didn't accept returns.

That was five years ago, and I hadn't seen him since.

"Hey, Steeg," he said. "How're you doing?"

"Holding it together. And you?"

He shrugged, and flashed a sheepish grin. "You know," he said.

"No, I don't. Why don't you tell me?"

His skin had a yellowish cast, and there were deep hollows under his eyes.

"I got a small problem."

"Bailing you out of the crap you get into is getting old."

"I know."

"If it's money, I don't have much, but I'll do what I can."

"No, no. I mean, yeah, it's money, but you can't cover it. I appreciate the offer. It's gonna take more than money to square things."

"Square what, Danny?"

He cradled his head in his hands. "Oh man, I really got my dick in a crack this time. I am so fucked, Steeg."

"You want a cup of coffee, something to eat?"

"Would you eat anything here?"

"Not if I could help it," I said.

"Besides, I can't keep anything down." He spread his hands on the table. I noticed the remains of a manicure, but his fingernails were bitten almost to the cuticle.

"Maybe there's something I can do. Tell me about it, and we'll see where we go."

Unbidden, Nick walked over with two mugs and a coffee-pot and set them on the table. He gave Danny the once-over and muttered, "Hump!" then walked away. I wasn't sure to whom the descriptive applied.

I filled Danny's mug, but he pushed it away and looked down at his hands.

"It's no big secret that I fucked my life up. But two years

ago everything changed. I hit the mother lode. Some guys I know, techies, started an Internet business and hired me as the marketing guy."

I was stunned into silence.

"I know what you're thinking," he said. "What the fuck does Reno know from Internet marketing?"

"It was exactly what I was thinking."

"See, I told you. Fact is, I know dick about it. But what I do know is selling."

Given his history, the jury was still out on that one.

"And," he continued, "I have connections. You know, where to find merchandise and shit like that."

"Was it hot?"

"Some. But most of it came from the inventory the dollar stores couldn't sell. The shit is warehoused and every month the distributor has to pay the storage fees. Money's going out and nothing's coming in. So, when I show up and make an offer, these guys are wetting themselves."

"So you buy it from them?"

"On consignment. This way we don't have to warehouse anything."

"And the distributor goes for it?"

"Like a fat man at an Atlantic City buffet. But here's the hook. At the site we put up, everything you buy is free."

"Free?"

"One hundred percent."

"And you make money from this?"

"Truckloads."

Danny had my attention.

"You can't imagine the shit people buy on the Web. Candles, stuffed animals that are supposed to be cuddly and cute but look like mongooses, gadgets that no one in his right mind would buy anywhere else. It's unfuckingbelievable!"

"Let's get back to the making money part."

"Sure. It's all about slippage."

My head was starting to swim.

"Slippage?"

"Absolutely. Here's how it works. You buy something for a buck and it comes with a fifty-cent rebate, which is the reason you bought it in the first place. Right?"

"Right."

"Okay. To get the rebate you have to fill out a certificate and send in a proof of purchase. You put your name, address, and UPC code, and send it with the proof of purchase back to the manufacturer's redemption center."

"OK."

"Now, how often do you fill out the fucker and send it back?"

"Never."

"Bingo! You're no different from anyone else. Depending on the price you paid and the value of the rebate, for everyone who sends the certificate in with the proofs of purchase, two, three, or even four people don't. Some get hit by a bus. Some don't fill the receipt out properly. Some lose the receipt, or the proofs. Some just forget about it. And if you get a couple a hundred thousand people visiting your website, and maybe ten percent buy stuff and you hold their money for a couple of months until you send it to them, it adds up pretty quick."

"It sounds like it."

"That's normally how it's done. But we added a new wrinkle."

"I can hardly wait."

He reached for the coffee, took a sip, and made a face. "This really is shit," he said.

"What did I tell you?"

Behind the bar, Nick glowered.

"Like I was saying, instead of charging you a buck for, let's say, a pen, we charged ten dollars."

"Seems pretty steep."

"Not when we promise to send you the ten bucks back in three months. Now you got your pen and your money back."

It began to make sense.

"Slippage," I said.

"Nail on the head!"

"It's brilliant," I said. "But it smells like a Ponzi scheme. You're paying three-month-old debt with new money coming in."

"Our lawyers said it was legit because we were solvent. We could have paid them anytime."

"What's the problem?"

"Everything was going fine when the goods cost a couple of bucks at retail. But then I overreached a bit."

"You got greedy."

"You might say. I got the company into high-price goods—TVs, sound systems—that I was getting from China, where they manufacture the stuff for pennies. When your minimum wage is a couple of bowls of rice a month, your margins kind of expand. At the end of the day, I'm taking a monster markup for product that I paid shit for. The problem was, instead of a buck or two a rebate, we had to pay out a couple of grand at a shot."

"Which you didn't have."

"Oh no, we had it. But our burn rate would have eaten us up in three months. Tops."

"So you do what every other business does. Go Chapter Eleven."

"We did, but it wasn't that simple," Danny said. "Turns out there was a group of people who had spent hundreds of thousands of dollars a month on the high-priced spread, waited until they got their money back, and turn around and sell the merch into the Third World."

"And this group is?"

Danny fiddled with a sugar packet.

"The Israeli mob."

"And how did they get involved? Wait, don't tell me. You dreamed up this little scheme and took it to them for a piece of the action."

"Pretty much. These guys don't fuck around, Steeg. They are truly the scariest people I've ever met. Make the Colombians look like fucking Good Samaritans. The guy who runs the operation—Zev Barak—gives me night sweats."

It was no wonder. The Israeli mafia had been operating in the U.S. for years. They were into drugs, arms dealing, bootleg gasoline, and anything else that could turn a buck. Even the Russians and the Italians steered clear of them.

"And what do you want from me, Danny?"

He shook his head. "I don't know."

"You want my opinion?"

"Sure."

"Go to the feds, agree to testify, and get your ass into witness protection."

"I tried that. But they won't have me. I got nothing tangible on Barak. At least nothing they want. Is there anything you can do?"

"How about I make a novena for you?"

After Danny left, I called the Minority Opportunities Bureau, the outfit Ferris worked for, and asked for the director. The operator connected me to Lou Torricelli. He wasn't in. I left a voice-mail message. Said I wanted to see him on a matter of importance. I gave him my cell number. I ran some errands and called him again. Another voice-mail message. The man had a thing about returning calls. Called him a few more times. Same result. I had the feeling Torricelli was ducking me.

I needed an in. I went looking for my brother.

I finally caught up with him at Nolan's Gym.

Nolan's, on Ninth and Forty-first, sat atop a Hasidic-owned discount electronics store. An interesting, if incongruous, juxtaposition of commercial enterprises.

The wooden floors were bowed and scraped of finish. Yellowed fight posters dating back to the 1940s hung on the peeling walls. A ring with very tight ropes sat in the center of the floor. Two munchkins in headgear, looking remarkably like Mayan temple pictographs, pounded the shit out of each other with great verve.

Nolan's counted several Golden Gloves champions, including me, among its alumni. On my big night at the Garden, I won in a walkover when my opponent, a tall, beefy black guy with diamonds in his teeth and the disposition of a reef shark, failed to appear. I eventually learned that just before the bout he was arrested and charged with a series of drive-by shootings.

Lucky me.

Nolan's other distinction was that there were no showers, making it arguably the most odoriferous spot in Hell's Kitchen. The sour aroma of fifty years of accumulated sweat hung in the air like swamp gas.

Dave was working the speed bag with metronomic precision. Small, pawing, rhythmic strokes performed with an economy of motion. His gray T-shirt was blotched with sweat. He had been at it for a while and was breathing hard.

"I heard you had a problem the other night," he said.

"The other three guys had the problem. I saw it as an opportunity."

That brought a resigned shake of his head.

"What's up?"

"I've got two things I need your advice on," I said.

"I don't see you anymore . . . Franny and the kids miss you . . . and you want my help," he said as the tiny bag thrummed under his fists.

I reached over and stopped the bag in mid-thrum.

"Very impressive for a man your age," I said. "But you've got to concentrate here."

He flashed a lopsided grin and motioned to one of his minions—a bullet-headed guy with a thick body and dull, tiny eyes—to fetch a towel. The towel came. Dave mopped his face and draped it around his neck.

"OK," he said, reaching for a bottle of water. "What's so important?"

I told him about Ginny and Tony Ferris.

"So, Ferris is black. That's got to be a thorn in Ollie Doyle's dick. And I'm sure the lovely Jeanmarie isn't too thrilled about it either."

"That would be my guess," I agreed.

"Both of them are open sores."

"Here's the problem, Dave. Ferris worked for the Minority Opportunities Bureau, a city agency."

Dave gave his thick gray hair a vigorous rub with the towel. "The M-O-B. Interesting acronym," he said. "Could be a clue."

"Could be," I said.

"So, all of Ginny's husbands worked for the city. Maybe she's a pension-digger." He smiled at his little joke.

"Anyway, I called Ferris's boss, a guy named Torricelli, and he's never around. I get the feeling I'm being avoided."

"You do have that way about you."

"It runs in the family. I could perch in his office until he's willing to see me, but it'll just piss him off even more."

"What do you want from me?"

"Any thoughts?"

"Why don't you go see Terry? He could set it up."

The mention of Terry Sloan's name made me wince. Sloan was Dave's buddy, and our local city councilman. That exalted position gave him more connections than a fuse box. The last time I was involved with Sloan was when he tried to make a quick buck from the 9/11 disaster.

"I would, but I'd need to be hosed off afterward," I said.

In the ring, one of the Mayans connected with a round-house right, knocking the mouthpiece of his opponent across the canvas and sending him into the ropes. A pink mist of blood sprayed from his mouth.

Dave pulled the towel from his neck, neatly folded it, and laid it on the back of a folding chair.

"Sometimes you've got to dance with the devil," he said.

"Sometimes," I agreed.

"Why are you doing this?"

"Doing what?"

"Getting involved with Ginny and a bunch of shit that you're not physically up to, and that's not your business."

"I've thought about that a lot lately."

"Come up with anything?"

"I think so. At first, I thought it would be great to be back on the hunt, doing something that I used to be pretty good at. But the more I thought about it, the more I realized I was bullshitting myself."

"There's another reason."

"Yep. Once, a long time ago, she loved me. It's got to count for something."

Dave nodded.

"What's your other problem?" he said.

I told him about Danny Reno's predicament.

"I heard about Barak. The guy's got razor wire in his head. What did you tell Reno?" he asked.

"I'd make a novena for him."

"Good advice."

Like Hell's Kitchen, the Hudson Democratic Club is an anachronism. With roots firmly planted in Tammany Hall, the club had deftly camouflaged itself in the pretty green foliage of Reform. But nothing had changed. There was still a Boss, and it was Terry Sloan. Terry had a piece of every deal in the Kitchen. Mayors came and went, but Terry hummed along, merrily plying his trade in the political bazaar, and fattening his bank account. Higher office held no interest for him simply because it didn't pay as well.

The club occupied a room on the ground floor of an unremarkable building near the Hudson River that Terry happened to own. The rent went from one pocket to the other. It was a large, bare-bones room with several offices around its perimeter. The precinct captains and other hangers-on who relied on Sloan for their no-show daily bread were dozing or playing cards.

My tax dollars at work.

Albert Mallus, Sloan's majordomo, bagman, and the éminence grise of the operation, intercepted me at Sloan's closed office door.

Mallus and I had a history. The long and short of it was we didn't like each other. At all.

"He's busy, Steeg," Mallus said.

"Fuck you, Albert," I said, brushing past him.

I opened the door to Sloan's office and walked in. Mallus was right behind me.

A photo display of Sloan's long reign graced his properly spacious, serious-looking office. There was the obligatory set of flags, and all around the room mayors, cardinals, congressmen, and senators smiled down from the walls. It made me want to gag.

Sloan was at his desk, his head lolling back in the chair, a dreamy look in his eyes. Kneeling in front of him was a woman with a long ponytail. Her head bobbed up and down.

"Hi, Terry," I said.

Her head stopped in the middle of a downstroke. She scrambled to her feet, shielded her face with her hands, and beat it the hell out of there.

"I guess this is what's called servicing the base, or is it the other way around?" I said.

He swiveled his chair around and I heard the rasp of a zipper. With that accomplished, he swiveled the chair back to me.

"Hey, Jake, good to see you," Sloan said, as if this were just an ordinary occurrence in the life of a public servant.

"Taking a break from the pressures of office?" I said.

He grinned broadly. "What can I tell you? They're drawn to power like a moth to a flame. You know how it is."

"Actually, I don't. Put on a few pounds, Terry?"

That bothered him. Getting caught in a Bill Clinton moment was nothing compared to having his weight become the subject of comment. He quickly buttoned the jacket of his banker-gray suit. Truth be told, Terry *had* put on a few pounds. His once boyish face had fleshed out, and his jowls had succumbed to gravity and begun the inexorable cascade over the collar of his starched white shirt.

"After a while, those rubber chickens add up," he said, giggling nervously.

"Doing the people's business requires sacrifices the average voter can't even begin to comprehend. Must be a bitch."

Sloan smirked. "What brings you here?" he said.

"Ever hear of the Minority Opportunities Bureau?"

His face pinched up in a fair approximation of deep thought, but I knew that couldn't be it, since it would be a first.

After a few long moments of coming up empty, he looked past me to Mallus.

"Albert, you familiar with them?"

"Yeah. They make sure the niggers and spics get a piece of the action."

Nicely put!

"We are talking about your constituents here, Albert, aren't we?" I said.

He jerked a thumb in Terry's direction. "His maybe," he said. "Me? I don't give a shit."

It was a short right. Probably didn't travel more than six inches, but I made a quick pivot and got my shoulders and hips into it. It was more than enough to send Mallus crashing to the floor.

Terry sprang from behind his desk and grabbed me. For a seriously overweight man, he moved pretty well.

"Come on, Steeg," he said. "It's just talk. You know how it goes."

"How *does* it go, Terry? Tell me."

"He doesn't know you like I know you. It was a mistake. Won't happen again."

Mallus tried to sit up and get his eyes to focus, but his senses were not where he thought he had left them.

Terry ignored him.

"Why are you interested in the Minority Opportunities Bureau?" he said.

I told him, then added, "I'm just poking around until a lead shows up."

Mallus had managed to climb into a chair. Surprising. I thought it would take him longer. No question about it, I was out of shape.

"Funny how everything that goes around comes around. Every guy in the neighborhood took a shot at Ginny, and she wound up with you. Then she dumps you, and now she needs you again. Go figure."

"The vagaries of the human heart are profoundly mysterious."

"Whatever. Now that you mention it, I have heard about the bureau," Terry said. "Run by a guy named Torricelli. The guy's an asshole."

I took that as high praise.

"Too honest for you?"

"Why do you have to be such a fucking pain in the ass, Steeg?"

"Family tradition. What's your problem with Torricelli?"

"OK, you're right. Too much of a fucking straight arrow, if you know what I mean."

I did indeed. Terry was intimating that Torricelli didn't

play his brand of ball. Even though he didn't return my calls, I was warming to Mr. Torricelli.

"How so?" I said.

"We've had a couple of run-ins in the past. I don't want to go into details."

I smiled sweetly. "Please do," I said.

Sloan looked over at Mallus sitting very quietly with his head cradled in his hands. His gaze lingered a moment, and then moved back to me.

"Gideon El had this construction company—all on the up and up—"

"Of course."

"And fucking Torricelli buried him in so much paperwork that Gideon couldn't get the thing off the ground."

Gideon El, né Randall Carver, the noted civil rights activist *cum* lowlife, had traded in his megaphone for an opportunity to bid on city contracts.

"What happened? The protesting business isn't paying like it used to, or was Randall just looking to expand?"

"Is there anyone you *do* like?"

"With each passing day, the list grows ever shorter."

"Look, I got a lot of shit to do. What do you want?"

"I want to see Torricelli, but he doesn't want to see me."

"What a shock."

"I need you to set it up. Dave figured you would help."

"Does that mean if I do it you'll leave?"

"Absolutely."

"Consider it done."

Terry Sloan called. My meeting with Torricelli was on.

In twenty years of public service, Terry had yet to introduce a bill in the city council, but he sure knew how to grease the wheels of government.

Louis Torricelli's office was on the sixth floor of a mud-colored hive of a building that housed a bunch of agencies no one has ever heard of.

There was no receptionist. I didn't expect one; city agencies are not particularly user-friendly. I stopped the first person I saw, a plump woman with a bad dye job toting an armful of file folders. She had the numb look of a lifer.

"Lou Torricelli?" I said.

She took a few seconds to decide whether divulging his whereabouts was part of her job description, a really important issue for city employees. And it drove me nuts.

The look on her face reminded me of the day Dave's wife, Franny, asked me to take her to the Department of Education to pick up her teaching license. Dave couldn't make it. The process should have taken no more than a few minutes, but there was a snag. Two typists were assigned the task of typing the certificate number on the license. One only did certificates ending in odd numbers, the other handled even numbers. Franny's certificate ended in an even number, and that typist had just left for lunch and wasn't expected back for an hour. As politely as possible, I asked Miss Odd Number to bend the rules a bit. Her reaction left something to be desired. I typed it myself. There was quite the commotion. Had Dave been there, there would have been blood on the walls.

Bad Dye Job was still thinking.

I waited her out.

After a few very long moments, she jerked the file folders toward an office in the back. "Over there," she finally said, punctuating it with a really deep sigh.

The nameplate on the glass-paned door read LOUIS TORRI-CELLI, DIRECTOR.

The door was closed. I knocked and walked in.

He looked up with a start.

My first impression was that this was a man who rarely smiled.

His office was quite the treat. Paint the color of day-old guacamole peeling up near the rust spots where the ceiling and wall met, a wooden desk purchased during Boss Tweed's reign, bookshelves heavy with thick reports that no one ever read. And behind the desk a smudgy window offering a delightful view of another mud-colored building stained with pigeon droppings. No wonder the man didn't smile.

"Whaddya want?" Torricelli said.

Perfect!

"Name's Steeg."

The look on his face said he was drawing a blank.

I passed him my expired NYPD photo ID and a business card.

He studied them very closely.

"You're not with the cops anymore?"

"It's a long story."

"Save it," he said, passing the photo ID back, but I noticed he kept my business card.

"Terry Sloan called?" I prompted.

That seemed to do the trick. His nose wrinkled up as if he smelled something bad.

We had something in common.

"Yeah?" he said.

Torricelli had a receding hairline and was going to fat, the ultimate destination for someone who sat on his ass all day.

"To talk about Tony Ferris," I said.

The color drained from his face.

"It's awful," he said.

"You might say."

"What happened? Who . . .?"

"He was beaten to death. The *who* remains to be seen."

"I called Ginny. I . . . can't believe it. Look, I'll help any way I can."

"How long has he worked here?"

"Fifteen years."

"Any problems?"

"With Ferris?"

"Yeah," I said.

"No. I mean . . . maybe."

"You're losing me."

"Not with Ferris. No problems there. Man did his job."

"Then with who?"

"I've been getting some strange calls lately. Ferris got them too. A guy with an accent. That's why when you started calling I didn't want any part of you. When you showed up, I figured this was not my lucky day. No offense, but you kinda look the part."

It was less than heartening to learn that I looked like a goon.

"Even though I'm here with Terry Sloan's blessing?"

"Are you nuts? As far as I was concerned, it cinched the deal."

Terry's stellar reputation had a way of preceding him.

"Ferris and his wife were getting threats too."

"He never said anything."

"Did you go to the cops?"

A fine sheen of sweat turned Torricelli's forehead glassy. He rubbed his eyes with a kind of resigned weariness.

"Are you kidding? He said he knows where I live. Knew my wife's name. Knew where she worked, even where my kids went to school. I don't need this shit."

Torricelli slid the desk drawer open and came out with a small brown bottle. He removed the cap, fished out a tiny white pill, and slipped it under his tongue.

"Look, I'm sorry I was short with you before. I wasn't being rude. I was being scared." He took a deep breath. "Here's the situation. I got three more years until the pension hits, and the last thing I need is to stroke out here. That would be like, you know, the ultimate indignity." His skin turned the color of the walls.

"We can do this another day."

He waved his hand. "I'm OK now. Just fire away. Ask me anything you want."

"What does your department actually do?"

"Do you have any idea what the capital budget for construction is in New York City?"

"Not a clue."

"It's big enough to make the Pharaohs, Incas, and Mayans combined look like a bunch of fucking mound builders. And that doesn't even include the cost of renovating existing stuff. Everywhere you look in this city, somebody's hammering, drilling, or laying fucking brick." He looked at the rust stains on the ceiling. "Except around here."

"The shoemaker's children go barefoot."

"Tell me about it. In the old days, most of the work went to outfits with sweetheart arrangements with the right guys in whatever administration was in office. See, they knew what the deal was. Administrations come and go, but these guys soldier on. Projects get proposed, bids come in, and the same construction companies usually wind up with the work."

"And BMWs magically appeared in the driveways of certain elected officials," I said.

"Sure, but one fine day all bets were off. In the sixties, the civil rights movement changed the equation. They pushed for federal and state legislation ensuring that minorities would have a piece of the pie, and they got it. And you know what? God bless them! Remember the riots? If I were black, I would have tossed Molotov cocktails right along with them."

I was falling in love with Louis Torricelli. If he kept this up, I could definitely see us picking out furniture one day.

"So the Minority Opportunities Bureau was created to ensure that blacks, Hispanics, Indians, Asians, whatever, got a fair shake. And if they were going to play fuckaround like their Caucasian counterparts who held the key to the lockbox for like a million years, more power to them. It's the American way."

"So the bids come in," I said. "You examine them and—given certain guidelines which I don't have to trouble myself with—you make sure that minorities are fairly treated in the bidding and awarding process."

"Bingo. But we also ensure that minority bidding companies are not only owned by members of minorities but also have a preponderance of minority employees in their workforce. Some of the incumbents try to get around the law by setting up subsidiaries or phantom companies. We sniff them out and basically fuck them over."

"But you don't completely get rid of them."

"Right. They're like fucking roaches. You step on one and the little fucker has already laid its eggs, waiting to be reborn as a new corporation under a different name."

"I could see where conflict might arise," I allowed.

"Yeah. Up to a few years ago, construction sites were turned into battle zones. You had blacks and Hispanics, armed to the teeth, bussed into the site and looking for work, and all hell broke loose. It wasn't pretty, and everyone concerned went about it all wrong. But at the end of the day, these guys needed jobs, and the dickhead construction companies and the unions were in cahoots to keep them out. My job is to prevent that from happening again."

"Did Ferris work on sensitive stuff?"

He pointed to files on the bookshelves. "Everything we do is sensitive. Where big money is involved, tempers get frayed real easy."

Torricelli's color had returned to what I guessed was normal for him, and he was breathing easier.

"Can you get me a list of projects Ferris was working on?"

He shook his head. "It's against the rules. But if I happen to leave a bunch of file folders on my desk and go to the john for a few minutes . . . With all the crap I got here, things sometimes go missing."

Torricelli was definitely one of the good guys.

"Is Ferris close to anyone here?"

"Lisa Hernandez, his assistant. But she's out today. Flu, I think."

"Do you have her number?"

Torricelli flipped through his Rolodex and found her card. He scribbled her number on a Post-it and passed it to me.

He pulled my business card out of his pocket and held it between his thumb and forefinger. "If I get jammed up, can I call you?" he said.

"Count on it."

He slid the card into his shirt pocket. "I appreciate it."

"One last question. What was your take on Ferris?" I said.

"Off the record?"

"Sure."

"Let's just say he favors restaurants with tablecloths."

"Hard to do on a city paycheck."

"I wouldn't know. I'm an Applebee's guy myself."

The next day, the number-one item on my agenda was to see Lisa Hernandez. That lasted for about fifteen minutes. What I really needed was an Allie fix. I called her. She was apologetic. Her morning was jam-packed, but a quick hot dog at the Plaza Fountain was definitely in the cards for lunch.

I arrived promptly at noon and found Allie sitting at the base of General Sherman's statue. She wore a denim vest over a Brooklyn Dodgers T-shirt. Her hair was pulled back in a bun. She looked troubled.

"You didn't get the account," I said.

She forced a weak smile. "No, it's not that. We haven't heard yet."

"Then what is it?"

She got to her feet, took my arm, and went for a big smile.

"Nothing, just the kind of a day that forces me to reexamine what I do for a living. I've got art directors who can't even draw stick figures, copywriters who think they're Hemingway, and clients who wouldn't know good advertising if it jumped up and bit them on the ass. My mother should have done the decent thing and drowned me at birth. Let's eat."

We walked over to a hot dog cart, ordered two with mustard and onions, and found a spot on the rim of the fountain.

"How's your life going, Steeg? Made any headway with your ex-wife?"

There were two ways I could have taken that remark. One, it was Allie's shorthand reference to the case. Or, two, the green-eyed monster had made an appearance. I went with the former. For now.

"I'm in what you might call fact-gathering mode now. Lots of people to see, places to go. That kind of thing."

"Really!"

Although she made a big show of it, I could tell she really wasn't listening. Instead, her eyes kept straying to Fifth Avenue.

"What's going on, Allie?"

She set her untouched hot dog down. "Did you ever get the feeling that you're being followed?"

"From time to time."

"No, I mean now."

"Care to expand on that?"

"Do you see that gray van?"

"Where?"

"Parked on Fifth Avenue. I noticed it last night when I left the office. Since then, every time I turn around it's nearby."

Sure enough, there was a gray van. It was a good way off, and the windows were tinted, so I couldn't make out the occupants.

"Could be one of those stick-figure-challenged art directors. And gray is the color of choice for vans. Hides the dirt."

"I'm not crazy, Steeg, and this isn't a joke. I'm being stalked."

"Well, why don't we find out what's going on. You wait here. I'll be right back."

I got to my feet and walked to Fifth. When I was about twenty yards from the van, the window slid down partway, and a hand appeared with the thumb up and the index finger pointed at me. Before the window closed, I clearly heard the word "Bang!"

With a screech of its tires the van was gone.

I walked back to Allie. She was trembling.

"I saw that," she said. "What's going on?"

"I don't know."

"Hey, man, I got something for you."

He was a black kid, about fourteen. There was a manila envelope in his outstretched hand.

"Who gave it to you?"

"A white guy. Gave me twenty dollars to deliver it to you, personally."

"What did he look like?"

He shrugged. "A white guy. You want it, or not?"

I took the envelope, and the kid melted into the crowd.

Ally stared at the envelope. "What do you think it is?"

I opened it. "Let's find out."

I pulled out a sheaf of photographs. Candid shots of Allie, DeeDee, and me.

"My God!" Allie said.

Someone had definitely upped the ante.

L isa Hernandez would have to wait. That evening I had an early dinner at a Hell's Kitchen red-sauce joint with Luce Guidry. She was all decked out in a narcissus-yellow two-piece suit featuring a gigantic strawberry pinned to the lapel.

I showed her the pictures. "Think it could have anything to do with the skanks I took down at Neon the other night?"

"Could. Even morons know how to operate a camera these days. Just point and click."

"Turn up any witnesses?"

"Not a one. Nobody saw anything, or too afraid to talk. Hard to blame them."

"The pictures might have come from another source."

I told her about Ferris.

"I always liked Ginny," she said. "Too damned bad, Jackson. I gotta give her a call."

"She'd appreciate that."

"Who's working the case?"

"Pete Toal and his sidekick. Guy likes to be called Swede."

She made a face.

"Don't expect much, Jackson. The word is, Toal is mailing it in. Just about everything he touches seems to wind up on the back burner. I guess that's what happens when you're nearing the end of your string . . . or running a game."

"Pete? He cuts corners but—"

"Pension ain't what it's cracked up to be. Easy to wind up in someone's pocket."

"Anybody have Toal under a microscope?"

"Not as far as I know," Luce said.

"Could the fact that he's a dyed-in-the-wool homophobe be coloring your thinking?"

When Luce and Cherise got married, Toal gave them a sex toy as a wedding gift. Thought it was hilarious. Luce didn't, and decked him.

She shrugged. "Could be."

"He wasn't the only one."

"No, he wasn't. Look, I'm just speculating here. But won't be the first time one of our brothers in blue played fuck-around."

On that happy note we called it a night. Luce went back to Cherise, and I went home, watched some television, and turned in early. I was awakened when my phone rang.

"Jake, it's Dave," he said.

I looked at the clock on my nightstand.

"What's wrong?" I asked.

"Everything's just ducky. Why?"

"It's five in the morning."

"Yeah, well, some of us work for a living. Had a situation, but now it's fixed."

The less I knew about Dave's "situation" the better.

"Anyway," he continued, "remember those two problems you laid on me?"

"Ferris and Reno."

"The former is still up in the air, but I might be able to help you with the latter," he said. "Meet me at Feeney's at eight. Breakfast is on me."

At eight on the dot I was at Feeney's. Dave sat in his customary booth at the back, reading the newspaper. Nick was at the bar, chatting with a guy I didn't recognize.

I slid in opposite my brother.

Feeney's was where Dave did business, and he always dressed for it. Today he was looking particularly spiffy in a perfectly tailored pearl gray, two-button number. A pale blue shirt and red tie with tiny yellow amoebas swimming all over it completed the outfit.

He jabbed his finger at an article in the sports section. "You see this?" he said, passing it over to me.

According to the headline, after years of eligibility, a star baseball player had just made the Hall of Fame on his last try.

"Yeah, I heard about it last night on ESPN. Apparently he had the stats and they couldn't prove he was throwing games."

"They should have talked to me. You know that condo I bought in Bal Harbour a couple of years ago?"

"Yeah?"

"Couldn't have done it without him. And they let him into the Hall. What kind of a message does that send to kids?" He grabbed the newspaper back and bâlled it up. "There's no fucking morality anymore."

"Do you realize how insane you sound?"

"Why? I didn't put a gun to his head. He came to me. And he isn't the only one. I just handle their bets. Besides, if it wasn't me, it would be someone else."

Illogical? Sure. Did it make sense in an inverted sort of way? Absolutely.

"You said you could help Danny."

"I did," Dave said. "Help's sitting at the bar with Nick."

I took a closer look. Nothing impressive. Baggy suit. Bad haircut. Sallow complexion.

"Who is he?"

"Kenny Apple. An accountant by training."

"I don't need someone to do my taxes."

Dave smiled. "I said, 'by training.' Actually, Kenny works for me."

"Doing what?"

His smile faded. "Anything that needs to be done," he said. "He is a little quirky, though."

"Quirky."

"Yeah. Kenny's an Orthodox Jew. Doesn't work on the Sabbath."

"And he works for you? Are you shitting me?"

"Uh-uh."

"Orthodox Jew and a lapsed Catholic. You can't make it up."

"Sounds to me like a marriage made in heaven," Dave said.

"Why him?"

"Danny has a problem with Zev Barak, right?"

"Right."

"Who better to grease the skids? Set a Jew to catch a Jew."

We were back to that inverted logic thing again.

"You want to meet him?" Dave said.

"Why not?"

He motioned to Kenny.

Kenny exchanged a few more words with Nick, slid off his barstool, walked over, and sat next to Dave.

"Kenny," Dave said, "this is my brother, Jake."

We shook hands.

"Do you know what this is about?" I said.

"Dave hit the high points."

"How do you think you can help?"

"I know Barak. Tough guy."

"That's what I hear."

"Russian by birth. Name then was Visnetzski. Came to Israel as a teenager. Went into the army. Golani Brigade. IDF shock troops. When Barak left the army, he got involved in the arms trade and eventually branched off into other, uh, businesses."

"Do you think you can help my friend?"

He shrugged. "I don't know, but we can try," he said. "Maybe he'll listen to me."

"And if not?"

He shrugged again. "I feel sorry for your friend," he said. "Do you know what they call Barak?"

"No."

"The Golem. Do you know what that is?"

"Not a clue."

"There is an old legend about a rabbi who lived in Prague. A pogrom raged in the city. Thousands of Jews were slaughtered. The rabbi, a famous mystic, went down to the riverbank and formed a man out of the clay. A giant. He inscribed a magical sign on his forehead, and the golem came to life. Now it was the rioters' turn to die."

"So, you're telling me Barak protects Jews?"

"Religion has nothing to do with it. Barak protects only what is his."

CHAPTER 13

I called Torricelli to see if Lisa Hernandez, Ferris's assistant, was in. She wasn't. Still had the flu. I asked for her address. Turned out to be Alphabet City, a neighborhood in transition on the southeastern edge of Manhattan.

When I had worked the area, the neighborhood was a slag-heap, a rickety place filled with rickety people. Dealers, hookers, outlaw bikers, and brain-burned junkies who boosted wiring, pipes, and whatever else wasn't nailed down. Sometimes from abandoned houses, more often not. And caught in the middle was a largely immigrant, working-class population hanging on by its fingernails.

Now change was in the air.

Heeding the siren song of cheap rents, creative types and urban pioneers had moved in and recalibrated the landscape. Alphabet City had become a very tony "in" spot, and the Prada and Armani crowd willingly coughed up a couple of thousand a month for apartments that were going for a fraction of that just a few years before. Lisa's four-story walk-up didn't fall into that category, so getting in wasn't a problem.

Her apartment was on the third floor, one of three on the landing. The marble tile floor hadn't seen a mop in years.

I rang the bell.

No answer.

I knocked.

The door to the apartment on my left opened. A short, round woman wearing a floral-printed housedress stood there.

"You a cop?" she asked.

"No."

"Oh, then you're *another* one."

I heard some shuffling footsteps coming from Lisa's apartment. A dark eye appeared at the peephole.

"Who is it?" she said.

I held my card up a few inches from the peephole and kept my voice low and friendly.

"Lisa, my name is Steeg. I need to talk to you."

"About what?"

"Tony Ferris."

I heard the quick snap of three locks being unlatched. Lisa Hernandez was a very careful woman.

At the last snap the door swung open, and Lisa appeared. She stared at the short, round woman.

"What the hell do *you* want?" Lisa said. "This ain't your business."

The short, round woman's face creased into a sneer. *"Puta,"* she said.

"Bruja," Lisa lashed back.

This had all the makings of an entertainment.

The short, round woman retreated into her apartment and slammed the door.

"What was that all about?"

"My day is complete. The bitch knows everybody's business. It's annoying."

Even in a white floppy robe and wearing no makeup, Lisa was a definite looker. Early thirties. Long, glossy black hair. A complexion that no tanning salon could hope to duplicate. Her eyes appeared clear, nothing leaking from her nose. Flu-less. Maybe this was a mental health day.

Lisa stared at me as if I were a hair floating in a bowl of soup.

"Come on in," she said.

I did.

She led me down a short foyer and into the living room. Her slippers made soft scuffing sounds on the hardwood floor. We passed a small kitchen, then a bathroom. The bedroom was off the living room.

The apartment was neat and furnished a hell of a lot better than mine. A very stylish cream-colored sofa, a couple of expensive-looking end tables, an Oriental area rug on the floor, and a flat-screen on the wall.

Not bad for someone who made thirty-five grand a year, tops.

She settled in on the sofa without offering me a seat. I sat down next to her anyway.

"What about Tony?"

Why beat around the bush? "He's dead."

She wrapped her arms around her thin frame and stared off into the distance. "I heard," she said. Her voice was flat. Resigned. After what seemed a very long time, she looked back at me. "How?"

I filled her in on the general circumstances, leaving out the more gruesome details.

"All I want is some information and I'll be on my way," I said.

"I've worked for him for over a year," she said. "He was always nice to me. Treated me well. I can't believe this!"

"Tell me about him."

"We had a normal business relationship. He's the boss. I'm the peon. I do what he tells me. But unlike most of the schmucks I worked for, Tony was a good guy. Really cared about what he did. I mean, the job isn't like saving the world, but Tony was like, y'know, into it."

"Into it?"

"Yeah, into it. Like it mattered."

"I would imagine that in the course of his business he stepped on some toes from time to time. I mean, when you're, you know, *into it,* hurt feelings are hard to avoid."

"It happens," she said. "I mean, getting a city contract is a big deal, even though you got to wade through a mountain of paper to even get your chance at bat. A lot of these contractors are just scraping by doing whatever comes along. So when they miss out on a job, a lot of them go under, and the losing bidder has to trade in his suit and tie for a pickax or a hod. Again. Are they pissed off? Sure."

"Would they be pissed off enough to retaliate?"

"Wouldn't you? I mean, most of these guys have everything they own locked up in the business. Their houses, cars, credit, it all goes up in smoke. Then their wives get up their ass 'cause they got to give up Bloomingdale's for Wal-Mart. It ain't pretty."

Fair point.

"Anything out of the ordinary happen lately?"

"Like what?"

"I don't know. Something on the order of making the hair on the back of your neck stand up. That kind of out of the ordinary."

Her voice tightened.

"Tony never mentioned anything," she said.

"It's funny you say that. Torricelli said that he had received some strange calls that bordered on threatening. Did Tony ever get calls like that?"

She twirled a hank of hair in her fingers. "Not that I recall," she said. "Look, I'm a glorified clerk. Too far down on the totem pole for stuff like that. The higher-ups like Torricelli, or even Tony, don't, like, confide in me."

"I see."

"Do you really?"

"Did Tony ever talk about his wife?"

She smiled. "The bitch?" she said.

"That's awfully harsh."

"I guess you didn't know her."

"Actually, I did. We were married once."

"Poor you."

"What's that supposed to mean?"

"Were you asleep most of the time?"

"In a manner of speaking."

She shook her head. "Guys are really stupid."

"No argument there."

"You all think you know everything, but you know jack."

Apparently.

"What am I missing?"

"Character is destiny."

"Could you elaborate?"

"What's the point?"

When I reached the street a gray van was pulling away.

Kenny Apple wanted to meet Danny.

I called him. He was holed up in a friend's apartment on Surf Avenue in Coney Island. Kenny and I hopped the N train at Times Square and took it to the end of the line.

During the train ride, it occurred to me that Kenny might be useful in other ways.

"Dave tells me you're an accountant," I said.

"CPA, actually."

"How does an accountant, and an Orthodox Jewish one to boot, wind up working for my brother in, uh, a non-accounting capacity?"

"Let's say it's the result of a life not well lived."

"Care to be more specific?"

He looked up as the train entered the 14th Street station.

"Why not," he said. "We've got another hour ahead of us. I was a gambler, a very bad gambler, it turns out. Bet on anything. And lost on everything. I had my moments here and there, but overall I took a bath. When I ran through my money, I used my clients' money. You know how it goes."

As a Master of Addiction, I did indeed.

"How did you meet Dave?"

"Through Nick, who held my markers. I was betting with one of his bookies. The guy insisted on payment. I couldn't come up with the money, so one day he brought along a shylock who offered me terms at the point of a gun. So, I agreed."

"Who wouldn't?"

"Then," he said, "I hit a particularly bad streak and couldn't come up with the vig. By this time, the interest and principal approximated the debt of a Third World country."

"And Nick was unhappy."

"Very. Nick sends the shylock and two very bad guys to see me. Figuring something like this might happen, I bought a gun. The shylock sets up a meeting in some deserted area right off the Belt Parkway, in the Gravesend section of Brooklyn."

"How appropriate."

"I thought so too. I got there early to scope the place out. I knew what was up. The shylock pulls up and the two goons get out with guns in their hands. I popped them before they had taken two steps. The shylock hits the gas, and he's gone."

"Very impressive. Where did you learn to shoot?"

"I didn't. Apparently it's a gift. The next one I hear from is Nick. This time the meeting is at Rockefeller Center, at noon. Plenty of people. We talk, and he offers me a job."

"To work off the debt."

He nodded. "And a little bit extra for me," he said.

"How do you square this with your religion?"

He smiled a wry smile. "Ultimately we all have to pay for our sins, don't we?"

"How would you like to do a little forensic accounting for me?"

"It would be a pleasant change."

I told him what I knew about the Minority Opportunities Bureau and the files that Torricelli had conveniently left on his desk for me to take.

"Would you take a look?" I asked.

"What are you looking for?"

"That's what I need you to figure out."

The train crossed the Coney Island Creek and, a few minutes later, pulled into the station.

When we were kids, Coney Island was the Steeg family's preferred summer vacation spot. Now, with about three months to go before the season started, Coney was like an aging courtesan who knows that no amount of makeup will ever hide the fact that her days were numbered.

Kenny and I picked up a bagful of hot dogs at Nathan's and met Danny on the boardwalk. To our right was the Parachute Jump, to our left the Wonder Wheel, and out in front, the Atlantic Ocean. We sat on a bench facing the Atlantic. It was low tide, and seabirds were busy pecking at the tidal sand in search of a meal. Out on the ocean, a stiff breeze kicked the whitecaps into high gear. On the beach, a guy in a Navy watch cap and a green windbreaker waved a metal detector, combing the sand for buried treasure. Every so often he stooped to pick something up, examine it, and toss it away.

"Let's start at the beginning," Kenny said. ·

Danny threw his half-eaten hot dog into a trash basket.

"I don't seem to have the stomach for food lately," he said. "Can't hold anything down."

"I understand, Danny," I said, "but you've got to concentrate here."

He turned to Kenny. "Steeg wasn't very big on the details. You're here, why?"

"Personally, I don't give a shit. But some people are interested in saving your ass," Kenny said. "Now, like I said, let's start at the beginning."

Danny repeated what he told me. He met some techies, joined the company as marketing director, and then everything went to shit.

"Nice story," Kenny said. "Boy from humble beginnings meets two techie whizzes working out of their garage and they start a company that goes on to rock Wall Street. The American Dream. Is that about right?"

"Pretty much."

"Do me a favor," Kenny said. "Stop pulling my pud."

"Whataya mean?"

"I mean, it's horseshit. Them I can understand. Why you? What qualified you to be the marketing director?"

Danny sprang from the bench and turned to me. "I don't need this shit, Steeg."

"Actually, I was thinking the same thing," I said.

Danny sat down, albeit reluctantly. "It was marketing and sales, and I had contacts," he said.

Kenny pressed him. "With who?"

"The odd-lot guys. You know, companies who handle distressed merchandise."

"More bullshit," Kenny said. "They already have plenty of outlets to move their goods. They don't need you." He turned to me. "We're wasting our time here, Steeg."

Apparently we were, and it was on me for letting friendship

blind me to Danny's line of patter. "Here's the deal, Danny," I said. "Either you stop the bullshit, or you're on your own. Your choice."

Danny dug his hands deep into his jacket pockets.

"OK," he said, "here's what went down. The techies. The guys who founded the company. I met them at a Texas Hold 'Em game Frank Geraghty was running in a loft in the West Village."

"The last I heard, Geraghty was doing a three-year bit in Dannemora," I said.

"You've been out of touch. He's been out almost two years."

"And apparently back at it. Some people never learn."

"Story of my life," Danny said. "The techies fancied themselves high rollers. I mean, back then the company was kicking off three, four hundred grand a month. Expenses were low, so there was plenty of money to indulge their Doyle Brunson fantasy."

"Why were you at the game?"

"I was the shill. Lost early and came back strong when the pot was right. Geraghty paid me a couple a hundred a night. When the techies showed up, we played them like fish."

"They had it coming," Kenny said.

"You got it. The first couple of times we let them walk off with maybe ten large. Made it look easy. Then we put the hammer to them."

"How much are we talking?"

"Quarter million. A lot of money even for them. Geraghty figured it was enough."

"But you saw potential," I said.

"Yeah. You know how it is when you're gambling. People

talk. Like to brag. Even when they're going down the tubes. Well, these guys couldn't shut up. Went on about how the two fifty was a drop in the bucket. Not even a month's worth of sales."

"And it got you thinking," Kenny said, "that there may be a way out for them."

"Uh-huh."

"Is this where China comes in?" I said.

"That's a piece of the bullshit I laid on them, but it never happened. I told them I could get them high-end electronics at a fraction of the cost, and if they pop it on their website it would move like a son of a bitch."

"So instead of candles that retailed for maybe ten bucks, they could be moving sound systems and flat screens."

"Exactly. And instead of three, four hundred a month, they would be doing ten times that."

"And they bought it."

"They did, the greedy bastards."

"Where did you get the merch from, Danny?"

"I knew some guys who heisted the stuff. I paid them ten percent and sold it back to the company at twenty percent."

"And you were on the company's payroll?" Kenny asked.

Danny smiled. "A guy's gotta make a living," he said. "We put it up on the site and the stuff flew out of the warehouse."

"But," I asked, "didn't the slippage go down?"

"Dropped like a rock. Those schmuck engineers had their heads so far up their asses that they forgot their business model."

"How did you meet Barak?" Kenny asked.

"Actually, he found me."

"How?"

"I get a call one day. Guy says he's seen the website. Thinks the concept is pure genius. Says he's been ordering lots of merchandise. I do a quick check, and he's right. Fifty grand an order. Says we can make even more money. Wants to talk."

· "So you meet," I said. "Without the owners."

"Yep. See, by this time I realize that there's just so much merchandise my guys can heist before it all blows up in shit, so I'm pursuing the China angle. If it works for Wal-Mart, why shouldn't it work for me? You got factories there that are churning out really great products and slapping brand names on them. And, since they pay their workers dick, cheap as hell. Why can't they slap my brand name on?"

"Sounds like a plan."

"And it would have worked if I had enough time."

"Let's get back to Barak," Kenny said.

"So we meet. And so far, he's been getting his rebates, every penny, like clockwork. But he's concerned."

"It's too good to be true," I said.

"Yeah. Wants to double his orders. Wants assurance that everything is going to be OK."

"And even though you know the business model is broken, you give it to him."

"Right."

"Why?"

"The assurance came with a price. He wants guarantees, he's going to have to pay for them."

"You're kidding me! You're hosing your employers, hosing your hijackers, and now you're sticking it to Barak."

"What can I tell you? It was the brass ring. Doesn't come around too often. And, as for Barak, I didn't know who the fuck I was dealing with. Who knew the guy's a psycho killer?"

"And now the greed has come home to roost," Kenny said.

"Hey, it was a shot," Danny said.

"More importantly, Barak wants his money," I said.

"It's beyond that," Kenny said. "He wants Danny Reno."

"Where are the techies?" I said.

"Beats me! Maybe the feds got them locked away somewhere, or maybe they cashed it all in and went where no one could find them. Or—"

"Maybe Barak has them," I said.

That possibility had apparently not occurred to him. His shoulders slumped and the color drained from his face.

"Now what?" he finally said.

Kenny and I looked at each other. I didn't have an answer. Neither did Kenny.

Out on the beach, the guy in the windbreaker knelt down, picked something up, studied it, and tossed it into the ocean with a cry of disgust.

During the subway ride back to Manhattan, Ginny called. The urgency in her voice was palpable. She was in town and wanted to meet at Feeney's. She wouldn't talk about it on the phone.

Ginny and her brother Liam were in a side booth when I arrived. Three empty beer bottles sat on the table. The fourth was clenched in Liam's hand. Ginny's hands were wrapped around a mug of coffee.

Liam Doyle always wore an annoying little smile that said he knew something you didn't. But this time Liam's stupid smile had company: a leather vest garlanded with chains, and thick-soled Grinders on his feet.

Fancy that!

It had been about eight years since I had seen him. It had been at his arraignment. The charge was lifting a couple of six-packs from a bodega. The trouble was, Liam was a regular customer who knew the owner, a cop named Figueroa, who happened to be working the register when Liam strolled out with his booty. The security cameras caught him, and so did

Figueroa, who leaped the counter and beat the living shit out of him.

I worked it out by convincing Figueroa that kicking the crap out of Liam was all the satisfaction he needed, and convincing the DA that someone as stupid as Liam would last about twenty minutes at Rikers. He got off with a conditional discharge, which meant he had to keep his nose clean for a year, and all charges would be dismissed. That lasted exactly two weeks. Lifting hubcaps was the charge. Interesting crime. Liam didn't own a car and had no interest in selling hubcaps. He just liked the way they looked on his bedroom wall. Little did I know Liam was an aficionado of hubcap art.

Ginny didn't bother asking me to intervene that time.

"Hey, Steeg. Long time no see," Liam said.

"Liam," I said, with a nod. "Keeping out of trouble?"

He took a swig of beer and leaned back. His stupid smile was on overdrive. "I got no troubles," he said.

"Glad to hear it. What have you been up to?"

"A little of this, a little of that."

Liam was one of those people who spilled his guts when ignored. I turned my attention to his sister.

"Ginny, you called."

Before she could answer, Liam jumped back into the conversation.

"There's a couple of things I'm working on," he said.

"I hope they work out."

"Yeah. No more sucking hind tit for me. Them days are over."

"Good. Everyone needs to catch a break."

"The way I see it, you make your own breaks. I mean, you see an opportunity and you jump on it."

"The soul of capitalism. It's what makes this country great."

His brow furrowed trying to make the connection. Finally, he gave up.

"Whatever," he said. "I got me a business."

"Good for you, Liam."

"Yeah, I'm a middleman."

"Really!" I said. "And what do you middle?"

"I'd rather not talk about it, if you know what I mean."

"I do. When you're in business, you can't be too careful. Trade secrets. Corporate piracy. The threat is everywhere."

"You got that right," he agreed.

We sat quietly for a while. He took another swig of beer and wiped his mouth with his shirtsleeve. "But seein' as you're family and all, and you know my partner, what harm could it do?" he said.

"I know your partner?"

"Your old buddy Danny Reno. We're into electronic equipment. Entertainment systems. Expensive stuff. I could fix you up with a plasma TV, if you're in the market. Insider price."

Danny Reno? Talk about six degrees of separation!

Liam heists the merchandise; Danny Reno fences it to his own company for a big payday, and then sells it to Barak for an even bigger payday, and promising a hundred percent refund. Liam, the brainiac, takes all the risks for pennies on the dollar. The guy was living proof of the axiom "Stupid is as stupid does."

"Thanks, but I don't have a spare wall," I said.

"Well, the offer stands. Anyway, for the first time, I'm making real dough."

"I'm glad things are turning around for you."

"It's like Jeanmarie says, 'If at first you don't succeed . . .' "

"Words to live by."

"I haven't seen Danny around lately, though."

"Probably out prospecting for more opportunities," I said.

"Yeah. I gotta hand it to Danny. The guy's always thinking."

"So it seems," I said.

"Well," he said, sliding out of the booth, "I gotta boogie. See ya, Steeg. And you," he said to Ginny, "stop worrying, OK? Steeg'll take it from here."

Ginny said nothing.

After he had left, I asked Ginny the burning question. "Take what from here?"

"I moved in with my parents, and Liam appointed himself my bodyguard."

"Now, that sounds like a plan. Protect you against what?"

She reached into her pocketbook, withdrew an envelope, and handed it to me.

"What's this?"

"Read it."

I did. Another death threat, but this time it was directed at Ginny.

D ave's house sat atop the New Jersey Palisades, a few miles north of the George Washington Bridge. It was raining, but when it was clear, the view was spectacular. From his living room window you could follow the line of Manhattan just about to the Battery. Dave had invited me for dinner and refused to take no for an answer.

Franny went all out. Candles on the table, a standing rib roast that could easily feed twelve, and molten chocolate cake for dessert. For the most part, the conversation was light and easy, but all through dinner Franny seemed distracted. So did Dave. At bedtime, my nieces wanted me to tuck them in and show them my scar. I did. They thought it was cool.

When I returned to the table, Franny was pouring coffee. "You showed them, didn't you?" she said.

"That's what uncles are for."

She shook her head in mock dismay.

"I understand you've been in touch with Ginny. Terrible what happened to her husband."

"It certainly was."

She sat down next to me. "I always liked Ginny. When you

two split, it was as if I had lost a best friend." She threw me a sly look. "I always thought you two would get back together."

"It didn't work out that way."

"But now, you know, she's single again, and she's . . ."

"Into her own life, and I'm with Allie now, Franny."

"Yeah, I know. But Allie's not really our kind."

I didn't like where this conversation was heading. "Our kind?"

"You know what I mean. Allie is really sweet, but she's . . . I don't know."

"Sure you do. Allie is Jewish, and your father was Puerto Rican. Now what?"

A blush tinted her cheeks.

"That's *not* what I meant! You know me better than that."

"I thought I did."

"What I'm saying is that Ginny is part of our world, with the same values. You know, a Hell's Kitchen girl."

"And Allie is?"

"Different. She's . . ."

"What's going on, Franny?"

Her eyes filled with tears. "She's going to take you away."

"I'm not following."

"From us."

"Keep this crap up and I'll walk off by myself. Allie is Jewish, and we're together. Deal with it. How come you don't have the same problem with Anthony? He's at Dartmouth carving ice castles with his WASP buddies. And you sent him there. Oh, I forgot. They're not Jews."

She glared at Dave and her voice rose to a shriek. "He dropped out. I wanted a doctor, and what I'm going to get is another killer in the family." She rushed from the table.

Dave stared at the tablecloth. The muscles in his face were slack. "Another killer in the family," he mumbled. "Sweet Jesus!"

"Did you have any inkling . . . ?"

"No."

"He never mentioned anything?" I said.

He clenched his fists. "Not a fucking word."

"Don't you ever talk?"

"All the time."

"Then how in hell did this happen?"

"Who the hell knows? Raging hormones, a search for his inner self, boredom. Pick one." He got up from the table and walked to the window.

"But you think it's something else," I said.

"Fucking kid. I think it's me. Who I am . . . what I do, embarrasses him. Dropping out of college is his way of telling me." He paused and looked around. "Franny's afraid he'll turn out like me. But she doesn't get it. He didn't grow up like we did. Didn't have a father like Dominic. Anthony's not like us. He's soft, like his mother."

"So, you're getting it from both sides."

"It's fucking relentless. Franny's tired of the life, Jake, and worried about the kids. She has a point. In this fucked-up family, ancestry is destiny."

I got up from the table and walked over to him. The rain streaking the windows cast the city in a muted, gauzy shimmer. "That's crap, Dave."

We stood quietly for several minutes, staring out the window.

"And then there's you. For a guy with one serviceable

lung, don't you think you're taking on too much? You were supposed to be the smart one. Where're your brains?"

"I've been trying to figure that out for years."

"Save your bullshit for someone else. You're my blood. All I got. If it's money you need, I can handle it. I got enough to set you up for three lifetimes."

"It's not money."

"Then what is it?"

"It's the only thing I'm good at."

"We're a helluva pair, aren't we?"

"A helluva pair," I agreed.

He pulled a cigar from a humidor sitting on a nearby table and went through the ritual of lighting it.

"How's the Danny Reno situation going?" he asked.

I filled him in on the scam and Liam's connection.

"Reno hired that fucking imbecile to pull his heists? Now, that's a really sharp criminal mind."

"That's not the only thing. I think Liam is involved with a skinhead group that I ran into at Neon. Skinheads equal racists, equal death threats, equal Tony Ferris. Not such a major leap."

"I heard about what happened at Neon." There was pride in his smile. "Even gimpy you really fucked them up."

"They pissed me off."

"A mistake they'll not soon repeat," he said.

"Do you know anything about these guys, Dave?"

"Like where do they hang out? There's a motorcycle repair shop on Eleventh and Thirty-fifth. You might find them there. Want some company?"

"Do I look like I need it?"

He patted my cheek. "I guess not. But that brings another thought to mind."

"Which is?"

"If you follow the dots, faint though they may be, Liam is connected to Reno, and connected to Ginny, who was married to this Ferris character. It's a stretch, but could Ferris's death be related to Reno's scam? Barak hasn't gotten to Reno yet, so he takes out anyone even remotely related, including their houseplants and pets."

"The thought had occurred to me."

"Hell of a family, the Doyles," Dave said. "Talk about the fruit of the poisoned tree."

"Except for Ginny. So far, she seems to have escaped the family curse."

"So far," he agreed.

"But when you come right down to it," I said, "screwed-up families are screwed up in their own uniquely screwed-up ways."

He smiled. "Aren't we special?" he said.

When I returned home, there was a message on my answering machine. Kenny Apple had set up a meeting with Barak for the next morning at Café Birobidzhan in Brighton Beach.

I looked out the window. The rain had stopped and the clouds had magically disappeared, revealing a climbing moon in an empty sky.

■

Brighton Beach, or Little Odessa, as the locals refer to it, is just up the road from Coney Island, and just about as stylish. I suspect the folks who developed the area had the seaside resort of

Brighton, England, in mind. Maybe that's how the neighborhood looked early on, but not anymore. Now all the signs are in Cyrillic, and it's packed with about a jillion immigrants from every SSR in the former Soviet Union. And preying on them was the Russian mafia, an organization that—according to Kenny—Barak was affiliated with when it suited his purposes.

The Café Birobidzhan was the only bright spot on a street that brought new meaning to the term "urban decay." The block hadn't seen a sanitation truck in years, the stores were tired and ramshackle, and overhead, the El cut through the neighborhood like a ribbon of scar tissue.

It occurred to me that Danny Reno was holed up just a few miles away.

Although the café hadn't yet opened for business, the large sign over the door was fresh and new, and it sparkled with gaudy chase lights.

"Do you have a negotiating plan in mind?" Kenny asked.

"Nope."

He rubbed his chin.

"Have you given any thought to what you'll give in return for Reno's, shall we say, safety?"

"Uh-uh."

The chin rubbing took on more urgency.

"Why are we here?"

"You set it up."

"I know that. But what do you hope to accomplish?"

"Make a new friend."

Kenny nodded. "I see," he said. "Should be an interesting meeting."

"I'm looking forward to it."

Kenny smacked the door with the flat of his hand. A very

large gentleman with thick features and a bad haircut, wearing about a pound of gold around his neck, appeared behind the glass.

"We're here to see Barak," Kenny said. "Kenny Apple."

The thug unlocked the door, and we stepped into the reception area. I heard the sharp click of the door locking behind us. The walls were covered in gold-flocked red velvet. Very tasteful. Autographed celebrity photographs dotted the walls. There wasn't one I recognized.

He motioned for us to turn around and patted us down. Neither Kenny nor I was carrying. It seemed to please him.

"Come!" he said, crooking a finger and motioning for us to follow.

We walked through the restaurant, past tables with upturned chairs sitting on top, past the restrooms, and stopped at a closed door with a sign that said Private.

Bad Haircut opened it and ushered us in.

Behind the desk stood a man with a shaved head and a narrow, hawkish face. His eyes were set deep under a slightly protruding brow ridge. He had no eyebrows. A silver-framed photograph of his wife and pudgy-cheeked son sat on his desk.

"Thank you, Avner," he said to Bad Haircut, who nodded and left. He turned to us. "Gentlemen. Please have a seat."

We sat on a sofa covered in buttery leather.

"Now," he said, "which of you is Kenny Apple?"

Kenny raised his hand.

"So," he continued, "you must be Steeg."

His voice was soft, with just the barest trace of an accent.

"I am."

"How can I help you?"

I pointed at the photograph.

"Nice family," I said.

Barak picked up the photograph and smiled.

"Thank you," he said. "They are my world. Everything is for them." He replaced the photograph on his desk. "So, I ask again. How can I help you?"

"It's about my friend Danny Reno."

"Ah yes. The elusive Mr. Reno. So, you represent him?"

"Yes."

He nodded. "It's good to have friends," Barak said.

"What will it take to square things?"

"A great deal of money, I'm afraid. With interest compounding at a rather alarming rate, Mr. Reno's debt to me is approaching a million dollars. Very serious money, Mr. Steeg."

"We both know that Reno doesn't have that kind of money."

"Does one truly know what is cooking in another's pot? I'm a businessman, Mr. Steeg. Nothing more. And Mr. Reno is a businessman. He understood the risks when he approached me."

"So, you both lost. It happens."

"Without question. But I relied on his guarantees. And now"—he shrugged—"I find that his assurances were worthless. I have no recourse to the courts, and to be seen as weak by my competitors is fatal. Your friend has left me with no choice."

"Look, there's got to be a way to work this out," I said. "Reasonable people can reach reasonable outcomes."

His lips curled into a smile. "I'm listening," he said.

I glanced over at Kenny Apple, hoping for a glimmer of a suggestion, or at least some inspiration, but he just sat there looking impassive.

"Let me think about it a bit, and speak to Reno," I said. "Maybe we can come up with something."

"Of course. Take all the time you need. But not too much. Unlike God, my patience is limited. And while you are thinking, I will continue to look for Mr. Reno and his associates. If I happen to find him, I will kill him and those who help him hide from me, in ways that will serve as an object lesson to those who even consider fucking with me."

"Are you threatening me?"

His lips stretched over his teeth in what passed for a smile. "In my business there are only facts."

That went well," Kenny said. "I don't know about you, but I nearly soiled myself."

We were on the train heading back to Manhattan.

"Barak is a very serious guy," I said.

"You think? Any ideas?"

"Yeah. Danny had better find a new place to live, pronto."

"Did you catch Barak's suggestion that Reno might have some money stashed away?"

"Hard to miss."

"Wouldn't surprise me," Kenny said.

"Me either. This whole thing is an infinity of scams. Have a chance to go through Torricelli's files yet?"

"I just started."

"Anything look promising?"

"You know, hanging around with you is turning into a job. When I have something, I'll let you know."

"Fair enough."

"Do you have any thoughts on who might have iced Ferris?"

"Not a one."

"Let me see if I understand this," Kenny said. "You were winging it when you met with Barak, and you're basically doing the same thing with Ferris's murder. Is that about right? No wonder the crime rate is on the upswing."

" 'Winging it' is too harsh. 'Letting it play out' is more accurate."

"I'm not following."

"Murder is the most ambiguous of acts, and the people who engage in it raise ambiguity to high art. What you think are facts are really idle speculations, and things are never what they appear to be. Getting to anything approximating the truth is all a matter of whether the Universe is benevolent or not."

"You mean the Hand of God."

"No. God and I have been on the outs for a long time now."

"Why is that?"

"Look around. If He truly exists, He should get down on His knees and beg our forgiveness. Each and every one of us. If we're all His children, that makes Him the adult, and He should know better."

He regarded my blasphemy with something approaching shock.

"It's the Universe, Kenny. And if you want to make the Universe laugh, make a plan."

"But without a plan you don't even have a fighting chance."

"You have just stumbled upon the voodoo that I do so well."

Kenny got off at 14th Street, promising to delve further

into Torricelli's files and divine their secrets. I got off at 34th Street to see a man about some photographs.

It had started to rain. Again.

■

Duck's Choppers, on the south side of Thirty-fifth, was wedged between a car wash and a diner the Board of Health somehow missed. A gray van was parked at a nearby hydrant. Four guys stood out front working on their tricked-out machines. One had a shaved head and a spiderweb tat on his scalp. They looked like they lived in a Petri dish.

"I'm looking for a fat fuck with a shamrock tat."

Three of them glared at me through sullen eyes. But the guy with the scalp art giggled. "That's Big Tiny, a guy you truly don't want to fuck with. You'd just be inviting a world of shit into your life."

"Thanks for the tip. Where is he?"

"Inside."

"Get him. Tell him Steeg is here to talk about peace in the valley."

The puzzled look on his face said he had no idea what I was talking about. "Whatever," he said, scampering into the building.

While waiting for Big Tiny to make his appearance, I reached down, grabbed a ball peen hammer, and turned every window in the van to splinters. The three jerkoffs stared goggle-eyed but made no move to jump me. Apparently, my special brand of single-minded lunacy was a new thing for them.

A few minutes later, Big Tiny ambled out.

His eyes lit on the van. And then they lit on me. There was the briefest glimmer of recognition before I hit him in the mouth with the iron. In a spray of blood and teeth, Big Tiny fell in sections.

I knelt beside him and spoke very slowly, but loud enough for his buddies to hear.

"It's time to drop photography and look into a new hobby. If I hear that you or your shit-for-brains friends were in the same zip code with anyone even remotely associated with me, I'll fucking kill you. Understood?"

The Neverland look on his face told me it would be some time before he understood anything, but I was sure his storm-trooper buddies, who continued to want no part of me, would fill him in on the details.

"By the way," I said, "tell Liam Doyle I said hello."

■

I went to Feeney's. Nick met me at the door. "There's a problem," he said.

"With the kind of a day I'm having, that's not a surprise."

"Ginny's here, and so is Allie."

A surfeit of joy beyond imagining.

I wasn't surprised. With Ginny back in Hell's Kitchen, the three of us were now stuck in the same tight geography, and sooner or later, we were bound to be tripping over each other. Apparently, that moment had arrived.

"Where are they?"

"Allie's at the bar, and Ginny's in a back booth having lunch. What do you want me to do?"

"I think it's time for the two women in my life to meet."

"Are you fucking nuts?"

"Some have claimed. Don't worry, I'll handle it."

"I can hardly wait," Nick said.

"And I'll have the corned beef hash."

I walked over to the bar and planted a kiss on Allie's cheek.

She beamed. "What a pleasant surprise. I was hoping to find you here."

"But the surprise doesn't stop here." I took her hand. "There's someone I want you to meet."

I led her over to Ginny's booth.

Ginny looked up, glanced at me, then took her measure of Allie. The corners of her eyes tightened. Allie was doing some appraising of her own. I had the feeling that neither was particularly impressed.

"Steeg. When did you get here?" Ginny said, never taking her eyes off Allie.

"Just now. Ginny, this is Allie. Allie, this is my ex-wife, Ginny."

Allie's smile turned hollow, but she handled herself with aplomb. "Steeg told me about your husband," she said. "I'm so sorry."

The tightness in Ginny's eyes loosened. "Thank you. That was kind." She scooted over to make room. "Please join us," she said.

Artfully done, especially the *us* part.

"I'm afraid I'm going to have to take a rain check. I have a meeting. Just thought I'd stop by. Besides, I'm sure you two have a great deal to discuss."

"Are you sure?" Ginny asked.

"Absolutely." Allie gave me a peck on the cheek. "See you later, Steeg?"

"Sure. We'll have dinner. I'll call you."

"Great! Nice meeting you, Ginny."

I slid into the booth.

"She's very pretty," Ginny said. "What does she do?"

"Allie's an advertising exec."

"How long have you been dating?"

"Going on six months."

"Is it serious?"

"I hope so."

Nick brought my hash and another beer for Ginny. She fiddled with her sandwich—tuna salad, I think.

"I can't bear living with Jeanmarie and Ollie, and I can't stand being alone. I think I made a mistake moving back."

"At least you have company."

"She and Ollie are not exactly what I had in mind." Her fingers slid across the table until they touched mine.

"What do you have in mind, Ginny?"

She leaned forward, and her hand covered mine. "It was good for us, wasn't it?"

I drew my hand back. "Let's talk about your marriage."

"I was about to say you don't know what you're missing, but I guess you do." She sat back in her seat. "I know. That was inappropriate. Shame on me. Now, let's get back to your question. Our marriage was good. Tony understood me."

"What does that mean?"

She pushed her plate aside. "Next you'll be asking me if I have an alibi for the night Tony was killed."

"Do you?"

"It goes back to your last question. Tony did understand me, but he also understood that I . . . sometimes indulge in other interests."

"By that you mean . . .?"

She took a dainty sip of beer and her eyes locked on mine.

"You know exactly what I mean. In fact, that's what I was doing the night he was murdered. I can supply you with the gentleman's name and address if you'd like."

I passed her a napkin and a pen. "I would."

As she wrote, she said, "He claims that I'm his first shot at adultery—what a horrible word!—and he's a little skittish about the whole thing. It's kinda cute, actually."

"Did anyone see you together?" I said.

The grieving widow giggled. "My bedroom is hardly a public place," she said.

"Did you mention any of this to Pete Toal?" I asked.

"Never asked. Guess he figured Steeg's ex-wife was pure as the driven snow."

Another myth shattered.

"And Tony was fine with this."

She smiled seductively. "I guess he figured I was worth it," she said. Glancing at my plate of hash, she added, "Your food's getting cold."

"Lost my appetite."

"Why, because I don't measure up to your exacting standards?" she said, her voice rising. "Don't judge me, Steeg."

"I'm not in that business."

"I know what's on your mind," she said.

"What might that be?"

"You're wondering if I didn't have *other* interests when we were married. Aren't you?"

As a matter of fact, it was exactly what I was wondering, until I realized it didn't matter anymore. Not at all.

I got up from the table.

"See you around, Ginny."

called Allie later that afternoon. She begged off dinner, mumbling something about a client meeting. The woman who divorced me now wanted to be with me, and the woman I wanted to be with didn't. Funny how life goes.

I was down to my dinner companion short list. On the off chance I might get an update, I called Pete Toal. Dinner was a swell idea, he said. He suggested Feeney's.

I tried to change his mind.

He insisted. For old times' sake.

I arrived a little after eight, and the place was packed. Toal was already there. Swede was with him. Kenny and Nick were deep in conversation at the bar.

I walked over to Toal's table and pulled up a chair.

He nodded at Swede. "Hope you don't mind. Old Swede here wanted to tag along."

"Not at all. How're you doing, Swede?"

"Good."

A man of few words. There's something to be said for that. Toal appeared to be enjoying himself. His collar was unbuttoned and his tie was pulled way down. His face was flushed, the only sign that he had already had a couple of Johnnies. Swede, in contrast, nursed a Coke and went for a very coplike look.

Toal reached for a menu, quickly scanned it, and put it down.

"So," Toal said, "what's good? It's been a while since I did anything but drink here."

"Nothing."

"You're kidding, right?" Swede said.

"Order something. Doesn't matter. It all sucks."

"What are you having?" Swede asked.

"Corned beef and cabbage."

"There you go," Swede said. "I could go for that."

"Trust me, it's shit."

"Why're you having it?"

"Reminds me of my mother's cooking."

Swede reached for the menu. Guess he had to find out for himself.

"Keeping busy, Steeg?" Toal said.

"In a manner of speaking. What's going on with the Ferris investigation?"

"Do we have to talk shop?"

"For you, it's shop talk. For me, it's personal."

"OK, we're nowhere."

I noticed that Swede was still studying the menu with the concentration of a scholar poring over Norse runes.

"How could that be?"

"Because we've got a caseload that would daunt Eliot Ness. Isn't that right, Swede."

I suddenly realized where the term "cop out" came from.

Swede wedged the menu between the napkin holder and the salt and pepper shakers.

"I think I'll have the brisket," he said. "How can you fuck up brisket?"

"The proof is in the pudding," I said. "Good luck."

He made a tentative reach for the menu again but thought better of it and drew his hand back.

"Sometimes you just gotta jump in," Toal said. "Anyway, like I was saying, in the past couple of weeks, Death hasn't taken what you would call a holiday. I don't know what the hell is going on."

"Let's start with the ME's report," I said to Toal. "Anything new there?"

"No. Ferris was beat to shit, but the cause of death was blunt-force trauma to the head. Appears that someone popped him in the back of the skull with a metal object, maybe a wrench. Several times. Hit him so hard that Forensics was able to recover some filings. Death was pretty much instantaneous. His last meal was endive and radicchio. I'd have gone for a steak."

"Was the murder weapon recovered?"

"Nope. We even had divers go into the river to look for it. The perp must have taken it with him."

So far, Pete was doing his job.

"Did you check the restaurant to see whether Ferris was a guest, and if he was, was he with anyone?"

"No one remembers. Busy night."

"How about the waiter?"

"In the wind. Probably an illegal."

Not so good.

"There was nothing, Steeg," Swede said. "We canvassed the area. No witnesses. No nothing."

There had to be witnesses. One area rife with opportunity that Toal and Swede should have followed up on crossed my mind, but I wasn't about to share it just yet.

Été was pricey, therefore an expense-account restaurant. If Ferris was there and used a credit card, the size of the bill and the number of entrées ordered should indicate whether Ferris dined alone. If he used cash, that fact alone should tickle someone's memory. It wasn't much to go on, but it was a start.

"Anything else?" I said.

"We interviewed his boss, guy named Torricelli, and a couple of his coworkers," Toal said. "The usual crap. No known enemies. Did his job. Nose to the grindstone kind of guy. Spoke to Ginny. Pretty much the same story."

"So, your theory is?"

"Well, like I told you initially. Lot of passion went into the killing, and the force of the blows tells me it's a guy. I don't think it's a coincidence that Ferris bought it in a known trannie hooker area. The way I see it, he ventured into the dark side one too many times. Wouldn't surprise me if he took his he/she sweetie to dinner, tried to break it off, and the guy went nuts. Happens!"

It did happen, I had to give Toal that.

"Did you interview the neighborhood regulars?"

"I left that up to Swede, here. Some things I'm just not good at."

I turned to Swede. "And?" I said.

"Showed Ferris's picture around, and came up with zilch. It's like a sisterhood down there. They protect each other."

"So, you're . . . ?"

"Like I said. Nowhere."

Swell! Now my list of suspects possibly included a guy in an evening dress. As I scrolled through my mental checklist, my cell phone rang. It was Luce.

"How come I'm the only one in the NYPD to have your cell phone number?" she asked.

"I didn't want anyone bothering me."

"Well, you certainly know how to screw up a birthday party."

"You gotta admit it was kind of fun. Just like the old days."

"That it was," Luce said. "Reminded me of the night at Crotty's Pub where you turned one of New York's Bravest into a battering ram. How many saloons did I have to scrape your sorry ass out of?"

I smiled at the memory.

"Too bad I'm a changed man, eating healthy and living right."

"If only," she said.

"What's up?"

"Braddock's been trying to reach you. Called you at home and you weren't there. Then he called me."

That was surprising. Gerry Braddock was my former boss, and someone who considered me a punishment from God.

"What does he want?"

She told me.

When I arrived at the Kings County Hospital morgue in Brooklyn, Ollie, Jeanmarie, and Ginny were leaving. Jeanmarie saw me and walked toward me very slowly.

She stopped inches from me. The skin pulled tight around her face, her eyes flat and unforgiving.

"My poor Liam is dead because of you, you bastard," she said.

Some things never change.

Ollie took her arm and tried to pull her away. "Let's go home now and prepare to bury our son," he said. "You're making a spectacle of yourself. There're people watching."

And there were, even at this hour. Swede was right. There was a run on death.

Jeanmarie wrenched her arm away.

"Get away from me, you worthless bastard," she said. "Let them see a mother's grief."

Ollie reacted as if he had been slapped. Jeanmarie turned her anger back to me.

"They wouldn't let me see my son's face," she said, spitting the words out. "And it's on you, Steeg. It's all on you!"

I didn't see it that way. This was on Liam and his choice of business associates.

Ginny walked up, mumbled a few words in Jeanmarie's ear, and led her and Ollie to a waiting cab. After they left, she walked back to me.

"I need a drink, Steeg," she said. "Now!"

We found a bar on Linden Boulevard. Ginny ordered a Jim Beam, straight up.

"Tell me what happened," I said.

"The call came about six. I answered. Jeanmarie was preparing dinner and Ollie was taking a nap. It was a cop. Figured it had to do with Tony. Asked if I knew a Liam Doyle. I said he was my brother. He said there was a problem. Didn't want to talk over the phone. Asked me to meet him here, at Kings County. None of it made sense."

Braddock knew Liam, and I guessed he heard the news over the wire and tried to contact me.

"And?"

"And we got in a cab and came down. I identified the body. It"—a shudder rippled through her body—"was awful! Whoever did it chained him to a car and dragged him through the streets like he was a piece of garbage."

Barak was good to his word. He had promised to kill anyone associated with Danny Reno, and Liam more than fit the bill. The snakes in my head awoke and began their dance.

"What's going on, Steeg?" she said. "Does this have anything to do with Tony?"

"I don't think so."

I told her about Liam's connection to Danny Reno.

"Liam got in over his head. Got mixed up with some very bad people."

"I don't believe this," she said. "This is all because of that little pissant, Reno?"

"It's also about Liam. No one put a gun to his head and forced him to work for Reno."

She drained her glass.

"The whole family has gone to shit. Tony. Now Liam. And who knows where Colleen is. What's next?"

Unless Barak got his hands on Reno, I had a pretty fair idea.

Ginny stared down at her beer.

"I know how you feel about . . . me," she said. "I know I screwed things up between us. But, at least for tonight, I don't want to be alone."

"I don't think so."

"Why?"

"It's not a good idea, Ginny."

"Please?"

So much for steely resolve. We went back to my place, and I held her until she fell asleep.

Later on that night, she awoke.

"What do we do now, Jake?" she said.

"Take your family and leave. Don't tell anyone, including me, where you're going. Just go."

"Are you serious?"

"Very," I said.

The next morning, after Ginny left, I called Danny Reno. I was relieved when he answered the phone, although I couldn't suppress the thought that if Barak had already paid him a visit, the killing would end there. For all I knew, every member of Reno's merry little band of heisters and their families had targets painted on their backs.

"It's me—Steeg. Did you tell Liam where you're staying?"

"I don't think so."

"Think hard, Danny."

"Why? What's going on?"

I told him.

"I swear," he said. "I never told Barak about Liam. How the hell did he find him?"

"Like God, Barak works in strange and mysterious ways. You had better call Liam's Nazi friends and tell them to make themselves scarce."

"Holy shit!" he said.

That about summed it up.

"You've got to get out, Danny. And you better do it now. Don't pack, just go."

There was panic in his voice. I didn't blame him. "Where? I've got nowhere to go."

I briefly considered offering him my place—maybe he considered it too—but quickly dismissed it as a truly bad idea. We were friends, but not that close. Besides, the last thing I needed was Barak in my life.

"Look, I don't care if you head for Epcot until this thing blows over. How are you fixed for cash?"

"I'm good. Got enough to last awhile."

"Perfect. From now on, you don't call me. Until this blows over, we'll communicate through Nick. Get a prepaid cell and leave the number with him."

"Do you think it will blow over?"

"You want honesty or bullshit?"

"Does it matter?"

"Good luck, Danny."

▪

Unless I came up with a solution, we both knew that it would end when he or Barak was dead.

I hung up and called Kenny. I was certainly giving my cell phone a workout this morning.

"Kenny? It's Steeg."

I told him about Liam and my conversation with Danny.

"You know," he said, "Epcot is not such a bad idea. The weather's good this time of year—not too hot, not too cold—plenty of restaurants from all over the world. And the place is clean. Good suggestion, Steeg."

"I was being metaphorical."

"Oh. So they dragged Liam behind a car."

"They did."

"Messy, but certainly makes the point, doesn't it?"

"It does."

"I told you Barak scares the shit out of me. The guy's got razor wire in his head."

"Scares me too."

"A definite sign of intelligence."

"Where are you on Torricelli's files?"

"About halfway through, but I have some thoughts, and some questions."

"Let's meet."

"It's Saturday. I don't work."

"But you picked up the phone. Isn't that work?"

"None of us is perfect."

I had enough problems understanding the observance swings among members of my own faith. I wasn't about to take on Judaism.

"We won't be working, we'll be talking. Look, I need to start making headway on something."

It occurred to me that I could kill two birds with one stone. It was close to noon and Été should be open, probably not for business—I suspected it was a dinner-only restaurant—but there had to be a manager there to talk to. After that, Kenny and I could meet.

"How about we meet at one, on the pier at Thirteenth Street?"

Kenny thought about it for a few moments.

"Fine," he said. "I'm not thrilled, but what the hell."

I was at the door when a truly chilling thought occurred to me. If killing Liam had been Barak's first move, there was a distinct possibility I was next on his shit list. I may not have had anything to do with the scam, but I was the only person on the planet who knew of Danny's whereabouts. I went into the bedroom, opened the drawer of the bedside table, and pulled out my Glock.

▪

I was right about Été. It wasn't a lunch place, at least not on Saturdays, but the door was open. Inside, a white-uniformed crew was mopping, primping, and setting up for the dinner crowd. Tablecloths billowed like snowy white spinnakers, silverware was carefully inspected, and thin vases were stuffed with wildflowers. Rather than a paean to chrome and glass and sharp-edged design, the decor was casual, a place to kick back and spend a comfortable evening. Été may have been high-end, but it kept its pretensions in check.

At the bar, a harried-looking man in a designer suit that had lost its crease was inventorying the stock. I went up to him and flashed my business card. It got his attention. He put down his clipboard and snapped to attention. I had a business card, therefore I was important. If I had pulled the same stunt at a diner, I'd have been told to piss off.

To keep the illusion going, I didn't offer to shake hands.

"Name is Steeg," I said. "I'm investigating a murder that took place outside of your restaurant a couple of weeks ago."

He looked properly contrite, as if Tony Ferris were a beloved member of his immediate family.

"I heard about it," he said. "How sad. We're not used to that kind of thing at Été. I guess the neighborhood still needs some, uh, work. By the way, my name is Stuart."

"Did you work the night of March 10, Mister Stuart?"

He smiled. "Just Stuart. No Mister necessary. That was a Saturday night, wasn't it? No, I didn't. I mean, I usually do, but I was ill that evening."

"So it would be a waste of time talking to you any further."

He nodded. "Colossal."

"What's your job here, Stuart?"

"I'm one of the managers. Assist the general manager. Work the desk. Greet people. See that things are going the way they should. The beverage manager called in this morning and said that he'd be late, and I offered to, uh, fill in for him until he got here."

"Who worked that night, Stuart?"

"That would be Richard. Richard Noonan, my boss. He covered for me."

"Will he be in later?"

He looked at his watch, a fat chronograph with a blue face and lots of bewildering little dials. It was a wonder he could lift his hand.

"Richard should be here at four. I'm so sorry I'm unable to help."

"Me too. Tell Richard I'll be back later."

"Absolutely. Have a good day now."

Well, that was singularly unproductive, I thought. I wasn't sure that Noonan would be any more forthcoming.

Outside, the day was a tease and the pier was packed. One of those summer days that pops up in March once every few decades. Warm, languorous, not a cloud in the sky, and barely a breeze to ruffle the surface of the water. A day filled with unexpected promise. The possibility that a foot of snow could be lurking a mere isobar away failed to deter anyone eager to shake off the winter blues and throw on a pair of shorts.

I walked out on the pier. A few seconds later, the unmistakable sound of gunfire shattered the promise of the day.

There were some panicked screams and a great deal of scattering. All except for one guy lying about ten feet from me with blood and brain matter streaming out of a very large hole in the back of his head. I pulled the Glock from the pocket of my fatigue jacket and went to the ground.

Suddenly, everything was quiet. The only man standing was Kenny Apple.

He walked up to the body and nudged him with the toe of his shoe. Satisfied that he was no longer a problem, he walked back to me.

I got to my feet.

"Where did you come from?" I said.

"I just got here. A car pulled up to the curb and this guy gets out holding a gun against his thigh. I figured he wasn't a sun worshipper."

"Good thought. Hell of a shot."

He shrugged. "As you are often wont to say, it's a gift."

"One of Barak's guys?"

"Presumably."

"I could swear I heard two shots."

"You did. I put one through the windshield, but the guy drove off. I got a piece of him, I think."

In the distance, sirens wailed.

"I thought you don't work on the Sabbath."

"I don't. But sometimes you've got to bend the rules a bit."

The sirens grew closer.

"For obvious reasons I think I'm going to leave now," Kenny said.

"I understand. I'll catch up to you later. Where are you going?"

"To synagogue. I have some explaining to do."

Lights flashed. Sirens wailed. Yellow tape went up like bunting. SWAT guys in Darth Vader gear prowled around looking for someone to shoot.

And out of the maelstrom stepped Luce.

"Are you all right, Jackson?" she said.

"I'm fine."

"What happened?"

"Beats me. I hear a shot and look around and see the dead guy."

Her eyebrows rose with skepticism.

"What are you doing here?" she asked.

"Taking my morning walk, and all of a sudden a gunfight breaks out."

"Save your bullshit for someone who doesn't know you like I do. Are you carrying?"

"I certainly am."

I removed the Glock from my jacket pocket and handed it to her. She sniffed the barrel, checked the clip, and handed it back to me. "It's a lovely story, but I'm not buying it," she said.

"That's because you're overly suspicious."

"Only when it comes to you. Whenever you're around, shit happens with alarming, and often fatal, frequency."

"What do your witnesses say?"

"Most of them were too busy scrunching up into little balls to see anything. And those few that did gave us a range of choices, from a six-foot gangbanger with a Crips bandanna tied around his forehead to a white guy with a limp. Would you like to weigh in on the subject?"

"Honestly, I don't know what happened. Except for the re-sults. For all I know, it could have been the consequence of some long-simmering dispute. Who knows?"

"Stop pulling my chain, Jackson."

"An old friend got mixed up with some very bad people who are looking for him. He asked for my help in the matter. This shooting might have something to do with that."

"So I was right, you were the target."

"Apparently, and I don't want to drag you into this if I can help it. They're not the kind of people you want around your picnic table."

"And their names?"

"Not yet."

"So the shooter was your guardian angel, a kind of Jiminy Cricket with an Expert shooter's badge."

"Could be."

"One of Dave's guys riding shotgun?"

"You know better than to ask that."

"You're wearing me out, Jackson. You know that, don't you?"

"What are friends for?"

"This wouldn't have anything to do with Liam, would it?"

"I think so."

"Then they are very bad guys indeed."

"Appears so."

"They dragged him behind a car, Jackson. Wasn't enough skin left on him to make a decent wallet. Don't want to have to call Dave and ask him to come down and ID you."

"I can take care of myself."

"Let's make that past tense. You *were* able to take care of yourself. Now . . . I'm not so sure. You can't be running around the city playing cops and robbers in your condition. Something's going to give."

"I'm as fit as a fiddle."

She shook her head. "Sure you are. I've got a question. Since Liam is in the mix, could Ginny's husband be in there with him? Ferris buys the farm, and then Liam. It makes one wonder."

"That it does. But I don't see it."

"Why? The way I hear it, someone took a pipe to Ferris. Mashed him up, like Liam. So, the means is different but the signature is the same."

"No. I know Liam was business. I *believe* Ferris was personal."

"Are you saying there was a sexual element to the crime?"

"Yep."

"Is Toal pursuing that angle?"

"It fits with his theory that a jilted trannie did Ferris."

"Where did he come up with that?"

"The neighborhood."

"That's it?"

"Pretty much."

"The man's a regular Sherlock Holmes."

"I'll give him this, though. I do think the doer was someone Ferris knew."

"Care to narrow it down?"

"I wish I could. My head is swimming with possibilities."

"Want to share?"

A partnership between cops can, if you're lucky, become something akin to marriage. Luce and I worked together for ten years. We completed each other's sentences, anticipated each other's thoughts, and built up a vast reservoir of respect and trust. And when you throw love into the mix, if that's not a marriage set to weather any storm, I don't know what is. The truth was, I missed her.

"You said you wanted to help."

"I did," she said.

"I can't bring you in on this, but if you want a piece of the Ferris investigation . . ."

She looked at me and smiled. "The things I do for love," she said.

We crossed the street and headed for Été.

O n the way to Été I brought Luce up to date on the Ferris investigation, and all of its possibilities and permutations. She had lots of questions and I had very few answers.

Inside we found Stuart, poring over the reservation book.

"How's business?" I said.

He flashed a harried smile. "We're overbooked," he said, "and I'm trying to make it all work."

"Is Noonan in?"

He pointed his chin at a whip-thin, prissy-looking guy with moussed hair done up in ringlets that were supposed to look natural but appeared to be pasted on. At the moment, he was addressing the waitstaff. At first, I thought it was a pep talk designed to rally the troops for the evening onslaught. I was wrong. Apparently, their recent performance wasn't up to snuff. It wasn't what he said that annoyed me—it was how he said it. Noonan seemed to take a special delight in strewing sarcasm like a demented Johnny Appleseed.

"Thanks for your help, Stuart," I said. "We'll take it from here."

Stuart went back to his reservations. We went to see Noonan. From his look of contentment, the tongue-lashing apparently went well.

I didn't bother with my business card. I had Luce.

"My name is Steeg. This is my partner, Luce Guidry. I was in earlier. We're investigating the Ferris murder."

"Ferris? I don't believe I know the gentleman."

"His body was discovered in your alley. Saturday night, a few weeks ago?"

"Oh, that Mr. Ferris. May I see your card?"

I handed him my card.

His fingers were very long and thin, and his nails carefully manicured and buffed to a high shine.

He glanced at it and handed it back. He wasn't impressed.

"This doesn't tell me very much," he sniffed.

Luce shoved her gold badge in his face. "Maybe this will, fuckhead," she said.

There's nothing like aggressive authority to effect an attitude change. Noonan took a few steps back. "I . . . see," he stammered. "How can I help you?"

I pulled out the photo of Ferris that Ginny had given me.

Noonan glanced at it. "He doesn't look familiar," he said.

"Look again," I said.

He did, and passed it back to me. "Sorry."

"Would you mind if I showed the photo to your employees?"

"This is not a really good time. As you can see, we're setting up for dinner. But, if you insist."

"I insist."

"Fine."

"One other thing."

He looked at his watch, sighed, and flashed a very unhappy look. "Yes?"

"We'd like to see your charge receipts for that evening."

"You must be kidding," Noonan said.

"Does it look like we're kidding?" Luce said.

"But that's impossible! All of the receipts are turned over to our accounting firm, and they're in tax season right now. I don't see how . . ."

Luce smiled sweetly. "Really? Then how would you like to see a full-court press by every inspector known to man? We might, if we put our mind to it, come up with all sorts of things, like rat droppings, underage drinking, undocumented aliens, or—heaven forbid—drugs. There are city agencies that have nothing better to do than make your life a living hell. How does that sound, Mr. Don't See How?"

Noonan's shoulders slumped. "Fine. I'll arrange for copies of the receipts to be delivered to you. Is that all?"

"For now," I said.

"Now," Noonan said, "if you'll excuse me, I've got a business to run."

"Ta ta," Luce said.

We did show Ferris's photo around, but no one recognized him.

Out on the street, the weather had taken a decided turn for the worse. The temperature had dropped about twenty degrees, and a biting wind blew off the river. New York weather is like living on the steppes; you never know what surprises are in the offing.

"I thought that went well," Luce said.

"Like it was scripted. Once we get the receipts, we'll have at least one question answered."

"It's a start."

"A pretty good one."

"Mr. Steeg! *Mr. Steeg!*"

I turned and saw Stuart bearing down on us. We waited for him to catch up.

He was out of breath. I knew how he felt. I get that way when I stand up too fast.

"What's up, Stuart?"

"I couldn't help overhearing your conversation with Noonan," he said.

"OK."

"He's an asshole."

"Yes he is."

"And you were right on."

"How?"

"There's a bunch of stuff going on in the restaurant that the IRS should know about. Most of the kitchen and dining room staff are illegal. Noonan has them kicking back a percentage of their tips just to keep their jobs. And I wouldn't be at all surprised if he's skimming cash from the register."

This was all very interesting, but it had nothing to do with me.

"Sounds like a charmer."

"Like I said, the guy's an asshole. But there's one thing you should know."

I had a feeling we were getting to the good stuff.

"What's that?"

"Since the murder, the cops have been here a couple of times to talk to Noonan."

"Do you know their names?"

"No. But there's another thing. Noonan fired a waiter

recently, guy named Roberto Banas. Been with us since we opened. Good man. Hard worker."

"Why was he fired?"

"Noonan wouldn't discuss it. What happened was, about a week ago another guy shows up. Looked kind of like a troll. Spends a little time with Noonan, and the next thing you know, Banas is gone. It's not right. The guy has family."

"Can you get me his address?"

"Sure."

I gave him my card.

"Just call me at this number," I said. "Now, let's get back to the troll. Does he have a name?"

"I didn't catch it, but Noonan seemed relieved when he left."

"Anything else?"

"That's about it. I gotta get back now. But I'll try to be more attentive from now on."

"I appreciate this, Stuart."

"So," I said to Luce after Stuart left, "there doesn't appear to be much truth telling going on here."

"I'm shocked, Jackson. *Shocked!* I was really warming up to Noonan. Who do you think the troll was?"

"Beats me. That description fits most of the men I've ever known. What's equally interesting is why the waiter was fired."

"We both know the answer to that one. Banas could identify Ferris."

"Bingo! Do you get the feeling that something is rotten in the state of Denmark?"

"Or in the city of New York. And what do you make of your old drinking buddy, the estimable Pete Toal? The son of a bitch has been holding back on you."

Allie hadn't returned any of my phone calls. It was time to mend some fences.

The receptionist at Bellknap & Hoskins waved me in with a smile. I was hoping for the same reaction from Allie. The door to her office was open and she was at her computer. I stood in the doorway.

"Hi," I said.

She looked up and her face colored. "Hi."

"Got a minute?"

"Not really. This copy is due ASAP, and I'm having problems with the headline. It's running too long."

"I'm having problems too," I said. "I screwed up, and want to apologize."

She turned away from the computer.

"You sprung Ginny on me. It wasn't fair, Steeg."

"I know. She was there, and so were you. Rather than skulk around like I had something to hide, it just seemed that it made sense to have you two meet and move on."

"The plan was fine. The execution left something to be desired."

"Ginny is my past. I'm hoping that you're my future."

"That was very sweet. Is this the part where I'm supposed to say 'Come here, you big lummox,' throw my arms around you, and plant one on your mouth?"

"It would be if *I* were writing it."

"I just don't know that I'm ready for that yet. You lead a very complicated life, Steeg, and so do I, but in a different way. I don't know what's going to happen when our worlds really collide."

"It could be a hell of an explosion. Plenty of fireworks."

"The trouble with explosions is, someone could get hurt."

■

In desperate need of some conviviality, I went to Feeney's. Dave and Nick sat in a booth drinking coffee. Kenny was with them, drinking water from a bottle.

I slid in next to Kenny.

"Why have a fucking phone when you never answer it?" Dave said. "And how come *you* didn't call *me?* You know I worry about you."

"Thanks to Kenny, I'm fine. Nothing to worry about."

"Actually," Kenny said, "there's everything to worry about. Barak isn't just going to go away."

That was heartening.

"Well, I'll just have to deal with it."

"It doesn't work that way," Nick said. "He had to know you're Dave's brother, but not in his business. Family is separate from business, and not to be fucked with. Sending his guys after you sends the message that all bets are off."

"Meaning?"

"He's going to move against me," Dave said.

"Is this some kind of twisted Machiavellian logic?"

"Nothing twisted about it," Nick said. "It's all about con-nections and opportunities. Barak kills you. It's satisfying, but all he has is one dead Irishman with lint in his pockets. But you're connected to Dave, and Dave has a thriving business. And that represents opportunity."

"I don't get it," I said.

Nick rubbed his forehead in disgust.

"What's not to get?" he said. "You're Barak's excuse. Lis-ten, he already told you he's going after anyone connected to that little scumbag Reno. You're at the top of the list. But he knows that if he takes you out, Dave will come after him. The odds of Barak coming out on top are fifty-fifty. But if he hits Dave first, the odds go way up. And if he takes your brother out . . ."

"Barak winds up with Dave's business," I said.

"Right. And he saves you for dessert. Got it now?"

"Shit."

"There's never enough for guys like Barak," Nick said. "See what you and your fucking buddy Reno got us into here? I told you he was bad news, ever since he was a kid plugging up water fountains at the schoolyard so he could sell lemonade. But you don't listen to anyone. Now we've got Barak to deal with. I wouldn't be surprised if that crazy heeb tries to bomb this joint."

A chilling but plausible thought. If he tried to kill me in broad daylight, why not bomb Feeney's? Take care of all the birds with one stone.

"How are you going to handle this, Dave?" I said.

His finger stroked the pebbly surface of his cheek, the ves-tige of a port-wine stain that had been lasered. This wasn't a good sign. When Dave stroked his cheek, reason was out the window and the killer was in the house.

"I'll handle it," he said. "May not be pretty, but I'll handle it. Don't worry about a thing. How're things going with Ferris?"

I delivered a précis of my conversations with Noonan and Stuart.

"Why would Toal lie? What's his stake in this thing?"

"That's a really good question."

"The answer has got to be money," Nick said.

"Terrific," I said. "But where is it coming from, and for what purpose?"

He didn't have an answer for that. Neither did Dave.

"While we're on the subject of money, Kenny, you said you wanted to talk to me about what you found in Torricelli's files."

"Not exactly," Kenny said. "The problem is, I didn't find anything. Everything looks kosher. There is an outfit, though, S&G Construction, that had been getting a lot of work for a while and then nothing."

"Could it be they're pissed off?"

"Could be," Kenny said.

I recalled the conversation I had with Lisa Hernandez. These companies are financed on a shoestring, and the least little blip could put them out of business. Motivation for murder? Absolutely, and worth looking into.

"Do you have an address?"

He passed it to me. It was in Queens, a borough I have spent exactly no time in.

Another item for my ever-expanding to-do list.

The next morning, I was in Queens, far and away the most bewildering of boroughs to navigate.

S&G Construction had its offices in the shadow of Shea Stadium, on a cobblestoned street that looked like chop-shop row. Every business except for S&G was involved in midnight auto parts, where the sum of the parts was worth more than the whole.

A couple of guys dripping with bling loitered out front. One tall and wiry with long, dirty hair pulled back in a ponytail. And the other, short and chunky with the beginnings of a beard, and tiny gold hoops lining his ear. Just your average, everyday morons.

I walked between them and reached for the doorknob. A hand grabbed my shoulder. It was Ponytail.

"Where you going?" he said.

This was going to be fun. "Move your fucking hand."

His grip tightened.

I grabbed his arm, spun him around, and drove his face into the door. Before the guy with the earrings took his shot, I kicked him in the balls. On his way down, I popped him on the side of the head. As I examined my handiwork, two thoughts crossed my mind. The first was that the older I got, the less patience I had. The other was, my docs were right. I needed more exercise. I felt better than I had in a long time. I opened the door and walked in.

A morbidly obese man sat behind a dented black metal desk smoking a cigar. He wore a striped shirt that fit him like an awning, and on his pinkie was a star sapphire as big as a pigeon's egg.

He nodded approvingly. "Nice job," he said.

"Thank you."

He pointed to a video monitor. "I got it all on tape. I could run you a copy if you like."

I shook my head. "Nah," I said, "it's stored in my book of memories."

The two morons burst in, and the fat man said something in a language I couldn't identify. Whatever he said did the trick. The morons did an about-face. The guy with the earrings still hadn't straightened up. Ponytail didn't look so hot either.

"Those two are my nephews. Their mothers are going to be very upset."

"I guess they were never taught manners."

"They think they're tough guys. You know how it is with the young."

"What language was that?"

"Albanian. Told them they were assholes. They'll learn."

"I'm looking for Arben Genti."

"You've found him."

"Got a minute?"

"After that performance, I've got as long as you need."

"My name is Steeg, and I'd like to talk to you about Tony Ferris."

"What about him?"

"Do you know him?"

"We do business with the city, so, yeah, I know him."

"Ferris was murdered a few weeks ago."

"Too bad."

"You don't seem overly concerned."

"I didn't know him that well. Why are you here?"

"I'm investigating his murder."

He held the cigar daintily between his thumb and forefinger, took a drag, and blew a smoke ring at the ceiling.

"So, you're a cop."

I didn't bother to correct him.

"What was your relationship with Ferris?"

"We didn't have a relationship. He was a prick."

"Threw you a lot of business over the years, though."

"Threw me shit," Genti said. "I bid on those jobs like everyone else. Won some, lost some."

"That's not what I hear."

"And what's that?"

"Not a lot of business went your way lately. Why do you think that is?"

"Why don't you ask him? Oh, I forgot. He's dead. Too bad."

Arben Genti was quite the charmer.

He mashed the cigar into an ashtray. "Are you accusing me of something?"

"Could be."

"Get the fuck out of my office," he said.

I parked myself on his desk. "All in good time," I said. "Tell me about your business."

He lit another cigar. Blew another smoke ring. I guess he saw I was in for the long haul. "You know what it is to be a day laborer?"

"Nope."

"You should try it sometime. Good for the soul. Not much else. You're either too cold, too hot, or too wet. Even when they're callused, your hands bleed, and your back hurts all the time. And you take shit from people you wouldn't let in your kitchen. And one fine day when your back finally gives out and you can't bring it anymore, your family starves."

"Doesn't sound like a day at the beach."

"Did that for years. Until I wised up. Now I'm a contractor, and I hire guys who work in the pit like I used to."

"And you would do anything to keep from going back."

He smiled. "Wouldn't you?"

"You mentioned that Ferris was a prick. Would you care to elaborate?"

"Not without a lawyer."

"Was he on your payroll?"

"That would be against the law."

"And you're a law-abiding citizen."

"That's why I came to the land of the free and the home of the brave. Nation of laws, not men. I learned that at night school. You gotta know shit like that before you become a citizen."

"One of the huddled homeless masses yearning to breathe free."

"Whatever. What's your name again?"

It's good to know that I still make an impression.

"Steeg."

"Right. Steeg. If I've been greasing Ferris's palm, why would he pull business from me?"

"Maybe his price went up and you decided enough was enough."

"Or maybe," he said, "Ferris found a higher bidder. Lots of maybes, but the question is, why kill him? He'd only be replaced by another guy with his hand out."

"You're from Albania, right?"

"Right. Small village outside of Tirana."

"If I'm not mistaken, didn't you folks invent the vendetta? If somebody stole someone else's goat three hundred years ago, his descendants would be on your hit list."

"Where do your people come from?"

"Ireland and Germany."

He laughed so hard his jowls shook like bowls of gelatin. "Talk about the pot calling the kettle black."

He had me there.

I called Luce from the Main Street subway station.

"Luce, it's Steeg. Where are you?"

She sounded preoccupied. "I've got something of a situation here. What do you need?"

"Some peace of mind."

"Fresh out. I'm on Thirty-fourth, in front of Macy's, watching a naked guy with two Tasers sticking out of his body, paying them no mind and pirouetting around like Nureyev."

"Sounds like overkill."

"That's what I thought. I've seen guys the size of panel trucks go down after one barb stuck in their backs. This skinny little guy just won't quit."

"How long are you going to be there?"

"Depends on how much electricity he can take. Maybe a half hour. Why?"

"I'd like to buy you lunch."

"At a real restaurant, or are we talking the usual hot dog stand?"

"A place with tables."

"You're on. Where should I meet you?"

I gave her the address.

"Did you say 150th and Third? That's up in the Bronx."

"I figured we'd look up Banas, the waiter at Été, while we're at it."

"You never disappoint," she said.

■

Banas lived above a cut-rate clothing store—the kind where most of the inventory is displayed on racks out front—and at eye level with the Third Avenue El. The El effectively killed whatever possibilities the neighborhood may once have had.

"Welcome to *El* Barrio," Luce said.

"No one should have to live right on the damn El," I said.

"Yeah, but look on the bright side. Every time the trains rumble by, he's treated to a new art show."

"That's why I love working with you. You always see the positive."

"Do you have a plan?" Luce said.

"Never without one. I thought we'd go up to his apartment and knock on the door."

"And then we'll have lunch? I worked up a hell of an appetite chasing Nureyev through the streets."

"As soon as we finish with Mr. Banas."

We walked up the stairs and I knocked on the only apartment door on the landing.

"Your plan is working like a charm, Jackson."

"What did I tell you?"

"Trouble is no one's answering. Let me try."

Luce knocked, with the same result.

"I think we need another plan," she said.

"Point well taken. Remember a couple of years ago the department worked that sting on guys who skipped their child-support payments?"

"Sure. Rented a room in a hotel and sent them a letter saying they won flat screens. Hundreds of the greedy little bastards showed up. Won't feed their families, but promise 'em a TV in their Christmas stocking, and they're Johnny on the spot."

"We're going to run a variation of that with Banas. Send him a letter, all official-like, and tell him I'm opening a new restaurant and that Stuart has recommended him for a job. I'll enclose my card and wait for him to call."

"That's all you got?"

"Pretty much. Either that or, perish the thought, keep coming up to the Bronx."

"Since you put it that way, it works for me. Are we about ready for the lunch part yet?"

We stopped at a small Mexican restaurant a few blocks away. We found a table, and I reached for the menu while Luce eyed the place suspiciously.

"Once again, you've outdone yourself, Jackson. This place is a shithole."

"But there are tables."

She pulled a handful of napkins from the dispenser and vigorously scrubbed the tabletop.

"Yeah, but I didn't know that they'd need to be hosed down."

I put the menu down. "I think I'll have two burritos stuffed with chorizo and cheese," I said. "What are you having?"

"A salad. Nothing else looks safe."

"Nothing ventured, nothing gained."

A waiter came by and took our order.

"Where were you when you called this morning? I heard a lot of noise in the background."

"Queens. Went to visit another possible suspect in the Ferris murder."

"My, you are a busy little bee."

"Guy named Arben Genti. He's a contractor, does a lot of city work for the Minority Opportunities Bureau."

"Ferris's outfit."

"Yeah."

"Why him?"

"For a while, Ferris threw him a lot of work, and then the spigot got turned off."

"How did you learn this?"

I decided not to tell her about the redoubtable Kenny Apple. Some things are better left unsaid.

"I hear things. Anyway, Ferris's boss, one Louis Torricelli, said he was getting threatening phone calls from a guy with an accent. Scared the living shit out of him. When Genti's name cropped up . . ."

"You figured he wasn't a WASP and made an intuitive leap and decided to check it out."

"Couldn't have said it better myself."

"Is Genti a possible?"

"Not sure. For some reason, Ferris screwed him. He has the accent. Albanian. And I have a strong feeling that Ferris was on his pad, but I just don't make him for this. Half the guys who handle city money are playing fuckaround with our tax dollar, but I don't think he'd kill someone over something like this."

"It's certainly enough to bring him in and persuade a friendly judge to subpoena his records."

"I know, but I'd rather let it simmer for a while."

"While it's simmering, he could be on a plane back to Albania."

"Nah! He likes it here too much. I think Banas could be the key. And until he shows up, I think we wait."

"What if he never makes an appearance?"

"Then we go to Plan B."

"Which is?"

"Sweat Noonan."

"I hate to play devil's advocate, but what if Banas doesn't show and Noonan has a sudden memory lapse?"

"Then we go to Plan C."

"You have no idea, do you?"

"Not a one. But something will turn up. Always does."

After lunch, Luce had to get back to work, and I headed to Été. As much as I wanted to wait for Banas to make an appearance, the idea of sweating Noonan, if only for the sheer sport of it, filled me with joy.

When I arrived, everyone was going about their jobs with a little bit of a bounce in their step. Imagine my surprise when Stuart told me Noonan was dead.

"A friend discovered the body," he said. "He went to Richard's apartment and found him in bed. Shot in the back of the head."

Noonan? I didn't see it coming. Maybe Luce was right, and I was a Jonah. Or, more likely, there was something I was missing. It was high time for the Universe to kick in.

"When did he find him?"

"This morning. Look, I've got to get back to work. With Richard, uh, gone, it's my show now."

"I need a favor. Noonan said he would get me the charge slips for the night Ferris was killed. Would you follow up on that?"

"Absolutely. Let me check with the accountants."

"Appreciate it. One last question. Have the cops stopped by to see you, you know, about Noonan?"

"The same detective who's investigating Mr. Ferris's death."

I called Pete Toal. Said he was winding something up and would meet me at the Lowell Fountain in Bryant Park in an hour. I was there in half an hour.

When I was a kid, the New York Public Library, at the eastern border of the park, was my go-to place when the world was too much for Dominic and he needed someone to take it out on. Back then, Bryant Park was a free-fire zone filled with addicts, pushers, and assorted bad guys. The combination of an iron fence and tall hedges hid what was going on in the park. Now low-growing shrubs replaced the hedges, the lowlifes were gone, and the park was back to being a park. It even had a carousel. But that cheery thought didn't lighten my mood. I found an empty bench near the fountain.

The longer I waited, the more I needed a drink. The dryness started at the back of my throat and spread to my tongue. The thirst was a symptom, not a cause. My old friends, the snakes, screamed to be watered.

At three on the dot Toal entered the park from Sixth Avenue. Swede was with him. I walked the few feet to the fountain and waited.

He saw me and waved. When he was in striking distance, I hit him in the mouth. He went down as if he had been poleaxed. The jolt of the punch traveled up my arm. Swede was too stunned to move.

"Wha—?"

I stood over him.

"Get up and you're going down again, you lying sack of

shit." I pointed a warning finger at Swede. "This isn't your business, so stay out of it."

Swede put his hands up and backed off.

"What kind of a game are you playing, Toal?"

His teeth were bloody and his bottom lip began to swell. He dabbed at his mouth with a handkerchief, saw the blood, and dabbed some more.

"Are you fucking crazy, Steeg? You just hit a cop!"

"Arrest me, and let your boss, Braddock, sort it out."

"I don't know what the fuck you're talking about."

A guy in a three-piece suit carrying a briefcase stopped to watch. Swede told him to beat it. He did.

"Allow me to explain. Either you're a bad cop playing out his string—a theory I prefer to go with—or something is going on that truly stinks. From the moment you caught the case, you've lied, or at the very least, left things out. Didn't cover the basics, and it troubles me. You were once a better cop than that. The other thing is, bodies seem to fall and witnesses disappear when you're around. How do you explain that?"

Toal slowly got to his feet.

"I'm gonna talk to you at eye level," he said. "If that's a problem, take your best shot."

"Go ahead."

"I'm conducting this investigation the best way I know how. If it doesn't meet your exacting standards, I don't give a shit. I don't owe you a fucking thing, much less an explanation. You can play cop all you want, but it's over for you, dickhead. It's been a while since you've been on the job, and with your health and all, maybe you're not thinking straight, so I'm gonna cut you some slack. But from now on, if you so much as fucking look at me wrong, I'm going to kill you. Do we understand each other?"

I noticed Swede watching with real interest.

"Nice speech," I said.

"I meant every word of it."

"I'm sure you did. So let me leave you with this thought. If I find that you're somehow involved in this—whatever *this* is—I'm not going to cut you any slack. You're on your own."

That evening I had dinner with Dave at a white-tablecloth restaurant in the Theater District. The place was filled with the after-theater crowd, and everyone seemed to be in good spirits. Dave had the rib eye steak, and I had a chunk of end-cut prime rib that filled the plate. We shared an order of garlic mashed potatoes and creamed spinach. It was as good as it gets.

"So," he said, "I hear you and Toal got into it."

"I think I broke a knuckle. How did you hear?"

"It's my business to hear things. It was stupid."

"Maybe, but it felt good."

"I'm serious here, Jake. The guy's connected."

"To who?"

"How the fuck should I know? But you look at his résumé—Anti-Terrorist Task Force, replaced you as one of the big, swinging dicks at Homicide—it doesn't happen by accident."

"He's a bad cop, Dave. And maybe more."

"Why do you give a shit?"

"Because Ginny asked me for a favor. She's family, or was."

"Great. I hear she's—"

"Save it. I know all about it. And I don't think she killed her husband."

"Why not?"

"I lived with her. She may not be as pure as Caesar's wife, but murder isn't in her makeup. Ollie, maybe. Jeanmarie, for sure. But not Ginny."

He shrugged. "Whatever you say." He took a sip of wine. "I sent Franny and the kids away for a while."

"Vacation?"

"Kind of. There's been a development with our friend the Israeli."

"Really."

"Yeah. I kind of rammed a stick in his beehive."

"How so?"

"I've got his kid."

"Are you shitting me?"

"He tried to kill you, didn't he?"

"It's not the same, Dave."

"Actually, it is. Just taking a page from history. It's what all those feudal kings did to keep peace with their enemies."

"The last time I checked, you weren't royalty. Why are you doing this?"

"Keep your voice down. Two reasons. Insurance. And something to trade. The first is business, the second is altruistic."

"I don't understand."

"From a business standpoint, his son is, as I said, insurance that he won't move on me. I want him to understand, if he fucks with me, it's going to cost him."

"You would kill his son?"

"In a heartbeat. Cut his fucking head off and send it to Barak in a bowl. How else would he know that I'm serious?"

"That's hard, even for you."

He rubbed his cheek and flashed a crooked smile. "Done worse, as we both know," he said.

"I don't know what to say."

"Nothing to say. That's why you're you, and I'm me."

"I can hardly wait to hear the altruistic reason."

"It's about you."

"Me?"

"And Danny Reno. You're my brother, my blood. And except for my kids, my only blood. I love Franny and would never hurt her or cause her any grief, but she's someone I met a long time ago. Not blood."

"You don't mean that," I said. "We're talking about Franny."

"I do, little brother. When you live long enough, there isn't a whole hell of a lot that surprises."

"You're not suggesting that Franny . . .?"

"Of course not."

"Then where's this going, Dave?"

"It's all about the pull of blood. I sent word to Barak that if any of his people fuck with you, the kid dies. I also told him that Reno is part of the deal. He's your friend, and if you think enough of him to put your life on the line, it seems to me that I've got to do the same."

This was monstrous. Even for Dave.

"Dave, don't do this. Let Barak's son go. I can handle it."

"Too late. It's done. I've got the kid. It's Barak's move."

He reached over and patted my cheek.

"Nobody fucks with my baby brother. It's a promise I made to Norah before she died. She worried about you. Wasn't sure you had the stomach to do what had to be done."

"Oh, sweet Jesus! Why do you make everything so fucking hard?"

"What are you talking about?"

"I mentioned Danny, and it escalates into a kidnapping. What in hell is wrong with you? Everything with you is over the top."

"It'll be okay. Sometime soon, Barak and I will talk. And when we're done, neither of us will be overjoyed, but we'll each walk away with something. He'll have his kid and a little more respect for me, and I'll have you. Reno is just a throw-in."

He threw some bills on the table.

"Blood," he said, "is blood."

The next morning my fourteen-year-old pal DeeDee called. She wanted to meet me for breakfast at Feeney's. I suggested a half dozen other restaurants. She insisted.

The acrid odor of cleaning liquid hit me as soon as I opened the door. While Nick looked on, two of his kitchen help, armed with buckets and rags, scrubbed the place down. It was hard to perceive a difference.

"Is this your once-a-decade tip of the hat to cleanliness?" I said.

"I hear you clocked Toal. Good for you. I never liked the prick."

"He was out of shape."

"And you with one lung. I also hear Dave filled you in on that other situation."

"He did."

"Kinda brilliant, if you ask me. With one move, that fuckin' heeb is hamstrung."

"Trouble is, they don't call him the Golem for nothing. I just can't imagine he's going to sit still for this."

"Where's he gonna go, to the cops? Come on, Steeg. He's got to deal with us. Got no other options."

"Let's say you're right," I said, "and he does deal. Who's to say, six months or a year from now, he doesn't change his mind and come at my brother with a vengeance?"

"We'll deal with that when it happens. Look, I gotta go check something in the back. What are you having?"

"Eggs over easy with two sausage patties, and a pot of decaf. And by the way, DeeDee will be here in a few minutes. Bring her—"

"I know, I know," he said. "Pancakes with bacon, extra crispy, and a glass of chocolate milk. I can't wait to see her. It's been a while. I'll bring everything on my way back."

I opened the paper and scanned the stories. Couple of suicide bombings in Iraq. Another CEO gets fired and walks off with a severance package worth over a hundred million. The price of oil is up for the third week in a row. Global warming expected to turn the Southwest into a desert. Three major leaguers caught in a steroid sting. Knicks lose. Mets win. Yankees split. *Groundhog Day*—nothing ever changes.

"Kinda depressing, isn't it," DeeDee said, tossing her knapsack onto the seat and sliding in next to it.

"Only if you take it seriously. You look terrific, kiddo."

And she did. With skin more gold than olive and cameo-perfect features, even in a faded Mickey Mouse T-shirt and jeans torn at the knees you could see the beauty she would become once she made it past adolescence.

"You don't look so great, Steeg," she said. "You taking care of yourself?"

"You bet. How's school going?"

"Except for analytical geometry, it's fine. I'm still waiting for someone to explain why a straight line needs an equation, and why it's so damn important. It's a straight line, for God's sake!"

"You're asking the wrong person. I'm out of my league here."

"That makes two of us."

"How are things at home?"

"Pretty good. He don't—"

"Doesn't," I corrected.

She grinned. "You never quit, do you?"

"What can I tell you?"

"Right now he doesn't bother me, and I don't bother him. We just share the same space."

"Sounds like a pretty good arrangement."

"It's really sad, if you ask me. Maybe, someday . . . What is it you always say, 'Hope springs eternal'?"

"That it does."

"You know, for the longest time I thought you made that line up."

"I didn't?"

"I looked it up. It's from 'Casey at the Bat.' But you never told me that Casey had struck out."

"You were too young to know the truth."

"That there's no joy in Mudville? Heck, I learned that a long time ago growing up in Hell's Kitchen. Anyway, let's talk about happy things. How's Allie."

"Fine."

"What's she up to?"

"The usual."

"You're not giving me much to work with, conversation-wise. I walk in, take one look at you, and see a mope. Then I bring up Allie, and I get the same monosyllabic answers that I used to be very good at. So tell me, what's going on? And if you say 'nothing,' I'm out of here."

"Allie is reexamining her options."

"Get out!"

"No, it's true."

"Why?"

"I'm not sure."

"Why not?"

"I'd rather not go into it."

"Come on! You're always after *me* to talk. Well, I'm fourteen. Not exactly a kid anymore. What's sauce for the goose is sauce for the gander. It's your turn now."

She had me there. "Fair enough."

"She dump you?"

"No. Nothing like that."

"Then what's the problem?"

"She thinks I complicate her life."

"How long have you been seeing her?"

"About six months," I said.

"Well, there it is. You haven't made the move, and she's getting antsy."

"The *move?*"

"Sure. The problem is, Steeg, you don't understand women. She's wasted six months of her life on you, and she wants a commitment."

Mercifully, Nick arrived with the food.

"How ya doin', DeeDee?" he said. "Damn, if only I were forty years younger."

"You still wouldn't have had a shot," she said.

He turned to me. "She has a mouth on her, doesn't she?"

"Tell me about it," I said.

DeeDee quartered her stack of pancakes, and then quartered them again. She cut the four slices of bacon in half and inserted a piece in each pancake section and doused the whole thing with maple syrup.

She looked up at Nick and smiled sweetly.

"I'm going to need more syrup," she said.

"You're kidding," he said. "Haven't you heard the word *cholesterol?*"

"I'm fourteen. Should I give a shit?"

Nick left to get more syrup.

"Now, where were we?" she said.

"Commitment."

"Right. As I was saying, if you want her, you've got to tell her."

"How come it doesn't work the other way?"

"You mean where she tells you?"

"Yeah."

"Because that's not the way it works."

She stabbed a pancake section, mopped it in syrup, and popped it in her mouth.

"Is there another guy in the picture?"

"No."

"You're sure?"

"Reasonably."

"Does that mean you're not sure?"

"Can we talk about something else?"

"You've got to step up to the plate, Steeg, even if you strike out."

There truly was no joy in Mudville.

Things were quiet during the next few days.

Allie and I had dinner, but nothing was resolved. Heard nothing from Banas. Ditto for Été's accountants. Didn't run into Toal. Dave still had Barak's kid, but Barak had yet to retaliate. I had three murders on my plate and was no closer to getting a handle on things than I had been at the beginning.

I figured it was time to stir the pot. Time to visit Lisa Hernandez.

As I stood at her door, the short, round woman stepped out of her apartment.

"You again?" she said.

"And a good day to you."

"She ain't here."

"You mean now?"

"I mean, no more. She moved. One day last week the truck came, and that was it."

Really!

"Did she leave a forwarding address?"

She folded her arms across her ample bosom. "Do I look like the landlord?"

"Hardly."

"The son of a bitch should rot in hell, the prices he charges for this dump."

"Do you have his address?"

"Whatever's on the rent bill. I make the check out to Clarkson Properties. Wait here and I'll get it."

Of all the possible reasons for Lisa's decision to split, fear emerged as a leading contender. But of whom, or what, was still an open question.

The short, round lady was back. She handed me a piece of paper.

"Here," she said. "You gonna talk to him?"

"That's my plan."

"Tell the thieving bastard he owes me a paint job."

"It's on my list."

"I tell you," she said, gesturing at Lisa's apartment, "I ain't gonna miss that one. Nothing but trouble."

"In what way?"

"Her and her boyfriends. They come and go at all hours. I got kids, and they don't have to see that kind of stuff. It's bad enough on the street, they don't need it here."

"So, Lisa was popular."

"I got another word."

"Were there any regulars?"

"A couple. One of them showed up a couple of days before she moved."

"Can you describe him?"

"Who knows? Besides, I'm not one to gossip. You want to know the truth, they all looked the same. Middle-aged, and grateful. You know what I'm talking about."

I had a pretty good idea.

"Well, I appreciate your time, and I'll certainly mention the paint job."

"You tell him if I don't get the paint job, Rosie Alba ain't gonna take his shit no more. And this time, she means it."

"You have my solemn word, Ms. Alba." I handed her my card. "Do me a favor, if Lisa shows up or you remember anything else about her boyfriends, give me a call."

On the way downstairs, I checked the realty company's address. Clarkson Properties. Park Avenue South at Thirty-eighth Street. I figured I'd stop by. It also occurred to me that this was the second time a mysterious gentleman had paid someone I planned on seeing a visit. In Noonan's case, it resulted in murder. I wished a better outcome for Lisa.

Barak was waiting for me in the street. He was leaning against a black Beemer. Two men were with him. And not your basic street thugs. These two were tall and rangy, and very serious looking. Naturally, I had left my Glock at home.

"Mr. Steeg," he said.

"Mr. Barak."

He opened the back door.

"Would you be kind enough to join me for a chat?" he said.

"I don't think so."

One of his men pulled a nine from his waistband and held it against his hip.

"I'd rather not discuss business in the street," he said. "Please get in. I promise, I mean you no harm."

It was a very persuasive argument.

I got in.

His men waited outside.

"It is written," he said, "that one cannot walk upon hot coals and his feet not be burned."

"And your point?"

"I have tried to shield the ones I love from the life I have chosen to live, and I have been successful. Until now."

"Believe me, Mr. Barak, I've had no hand in what happened to your son, and I am truly sorry it's come to this."

"I do believe you. A child is a very precious thing, Mr. Steeg," he said. "Ari is my only child, his mother's delight. Do you know how old he is, Mr. Steeg?"

"I don't," I said.

"Fourteen. A baby. Taken from his mother and forced to endure a horror I tried to spare him."

"I had no part in this."

"And this friend of yours, this Reno. Is his life worth my son's?"

"No."

"That is an honest answer, and you have my respect. Yet your friend will benefit if the trade is made."

"Yes, he will."

"Is that fair?"

"No. It's just a fact."

"You are loyal to your friend?"

"Yes."

"And your brother is loyal to you. He is also loyal to his son, Anthony, and his wife and daughters. Anthony is a fine boy, well educated."

A cold chill rippled through my body.

"Is there a threat in there somewhere?"

"You answered me honestly, so I will do the same. Of

course there's a threat. But will I act on it? Not unless I am forced to. You see, Mr. Steeg, there are rules in our business. Your brother has acted rashly and broken the rules, but I am not your brother."

"Why are you telling me this?"

"I will meet with your brother, and we will resolve the differences between us. But for every tear my son has shed there will be a reckoning. Tell him that, Mr. Steeg."

called Dave and delivered Barak's message. It didn't seem to faze him. Everything was working out, he said. Under control. I wondered which voice in his head he was listening to. Next, figuring I'd save a trip to Clarkson Properties, I gave Lou Torricelli a ring.

He answered the phone.

"Lou, this is Steeg. Do you have a new address for Lisa Hernandez?"

"What's wrong with her old address, the one I gave you?"

"She moved. Didn't she mention that?"

"No. She came in about a week ago and put in for a leave of absence, but didn't say anything about moving."

I guess it was fair to assume she didn't leave a forwarding address.

"Why would she take a leave? Strange, isn't it?"

"Not really. I'm sure Ferris's death affected her. Lisa is like that. Very sensitive."

Maybe I missed that side of her.

My next stop was Clarkson Properties, where I struck out twice more. Despite my vaunted powers of persuasion, they refused to provide Lisa's forwarding address. Something about confidentiality. And, worse yet, they were completely unmoved by Rosie Alba's request for a paint job.

Drastic times call for drastic measures. I called Kenny Apple and asked him to meet me at Feeney's. He was out front when I arrived.

"I need a favor, Kenny," I said.

"I'm still depressed over the last one I did for you. Killing someone on the Sabbath is a really big deal."

"But you saved a life—mine—and he who saves a life, it's as if he saved a whole world."

He thought about it for a few moments. "Not a bad point," he said.

"And this favor doesn't involve bloodshed. Let's talk about it over a cup of coffee."

He followed me inside, and we found a back booth. Nick brought a pot of coffee for me, and a bottled water for Kenny.

"What do you need?" he said.

"A young lady, named Lisa Hernandez, recently moved from her apartment to parts unknown. I need her new address."

A look of befuddled wonder spread across his face.

"Last Saturday I iced a guy for you, and now I'm a locator of lost persons? Are you serious?"

"Entirely."

"I can't believe this is what I've come to. Thank God my mother is dead, so she doesn't have to see this. Look, she must have left a forwarding address with someone."

"Afraid not. I've checked. The woman has purposely tried to disappear."

"I envy her," Kenny said. "Do you have any idea how many moving companies there are in this city?"

"More than you can shake a stick at, I suspect."

"And that's probably a conservative estimate. You'll be tying me up for weeks."

"Days. I really need it quickly."

"Of course you do." He held out his hand. "Give me the address."

I scribbled it on a napkin.

"When was this?"

"About a week ago," I said.

He slid out of the booth. "I'll get back to you."

"Happy hunting," I said.

Nick walked over. "Why's Kenny so down in the mouth?" he said.

I told him.

"I don't blame him," Nick said. "You're underutilizing his talents. You should have come to me first. If it's a forwarding address you need, I can get it."

"How?"

"Send a couple of guys over to that realty office and mention that a few of their buildings might wind up singed if they don't hand it over."

"Seems a bit heavy-handed."

"Yeah, but it's an attention getter."

"I don't think so."

"There is another way," Nick said. "Maybe not as dramatic, but probably as effective."

"What's that?"

"Union problems. My guys might mention that they could have some problems with oil deliveries, or their building supers might suddenly all get sick at the same time. Lots of ways to skin this cat."

I was warming to his approach.

"It just might work," I said.

"Oh, it'll work. I guarantee it. The tenants are inside with no hot water, while outside the garbage piles up. Sort of like a two-for-one deal."

"Let's do it. And while they're at it, have your guys remind them that Rosie Alba is due a paint job."

"Who in hell is Rosie Alba?"

"A friend who needs a paint job."

"Does she have any color in mind?"

"Just do it."

"OK," Nick said. "I'll call Kenny and tell him the situation is fixed. Should make him happy. But I got to tell you, I still like the more direct approach."

His gaze strayed to the front of the saloon. "There's a guy standing out there," he said. "Looks kind of familiar. Been out there for a while sneaking peeks at you. Know him?"

I did. It was Swede.

"I'll be back in a few minutes," I said.

I walked outside. Toal was nowhere in sight. Surprising.

"What brings you here, Swede?"

"Let's take a walk," he said. "I'd like a few minutes of your time."

"Where's Pete?"

"Back at the precinct. Paperwork."

We walked toward the river.

"I hear you were born here," he said.

"Couple of blocks over."

"And your dad was a cop too."

"Detective."

"So, your basic cop family. Except for your brother."

I wondered where this was going.

He looked up at the scaffolding garlanding the buildings.

"Everything's changing, isn't it?" he said. "Gonna need a scorecard to keep everything straight."

A Department of Sanitation sweeper rolled by. Small bits of trash churned in its wake.

"I hear this was a tough neighborhood once," he said. "Now look at it."

"It still is. You're just looking in the wrong places."

"Maybe," he said. "Is the park still on Twelfth, or have they built an office tower on the site?"

"Clinton Park? Not yet."

"Good. Let's sit awhile. There's something I want to talk to you about."

For the next couple of blocks, Swede was silent. The park was empty when we arrived. Swede stopped at the first bench we came to and sat down. I joined him.

A tug nosed a barge downriver.

"Very peaceful spot," he said. "Set far enough away from the traffic so you don't hear the noise."

"A regular Garden of Eden."

"Peace and quiet. It's nice. I wonder what this place looked like before we came along and fucked it up."

"It was all meadows and streams and flowering plants, as far as the eye could see. The Dutch called it Bloemendael, the Vale of Blooming Flowers."

"How do you know this?"

"When you love something—a place, a woman—you make it your business to know."

"How did it go from Bloemendael to Hell's Kitchen?"

"Progress. The Industrial Revolution crossed the Atlantic. Some robber baron wanted to build a railroad along the Hudson, and the Irish and Germans poured in. It didn't take long before you had a slum to beat all slums. There was a saloon on every block and chimneys pouring shit into the sky. What better name than Hell's Kitchen?"

"We do tend to screw things up, don't we?"

"I don't want to cut the history lesson short, but you said you had something you wanted to talk about."

"I'll get right to the point," he said. "You're a hothead, Steeg. A loose cannon. And you're fucking things up. So back off, and leave well enough alone."

"Could you be a little more specific?"

"No. Just take it as some friendly advice."

"Why? You're not my friend. And to tell you the truth, the more I see you, the less I like."

"What are you going to do, slug me, too?"

"The thought crossed my mind."

"Did anyone ever tell you that you could fuck up a wet dream? We got something going here, and that's all I'm going to say. So back the hell off before you get caught in the crossfire."

"Are you threatening me?"

"It is what it is, and I can't say any more. In fact, I'm done here."

"I want to thank you."

"For what?"

"Confirming that you and Toal are on someone's pad. At first, I thought it was just Toal. Who is it, Swede? Who are you carrying water for?"

He got to his feet, and shook his head and smiled.

"Why did I know this would be a waste of time?" he said.

After Swede left, I called Luce and filled her in on the conversation.

"I told you," she said. "Toal's running some kind of a game. If I were you, I'd listen to Swede. I keep telling you that you don't need any more shit in your life, but it's like I'm talking to a wall."

Good advice, but we both knew I wasn't going to take it.

left the park wiser but less happy, and went home. A question nagged at me. Who was the puppet master? And what was at stake? The only thing I knew with a high degree of certainty was that sending Swede wasn't Toal's idea. Subtlety wasn't in his bag of tricks.

I climbed the stairs to my apartment. When I reached my landing, I heard the tramp of footsteps coming down the stairs from above.

It was Danny Reno.

A sudden weariness came over me. "Where did you come from?" I said.

"The roof. Been waiting for you. I saw you walking on the street and turn into the building."

"What are you doing here?"

"Thought maybe you'd bring me up to date on what's going on."

"That's what phones are for," I said. "Are you nuts, or do you have a death wish? Barak is still out there looking for you."

Either way, he looked awful. His skin had a yellowish tinge, his eyes were dull and lusterless, and he hadn't shaved since the last time I saw him.

"Are you going to invite me in?" he asked.

I unlocked the door to my apartment and held it open. "Sure," I said, "but don't plan on making it permanent."

He flopped on the sofa. "I understand," he said.

I went into the kitchen. "You want something to eat?"

"Nah. Just a soda, if you have it."

I brought in a can of Diet Coke and handed it to him.

"Why are you here, Danny?"

He held the can to his temple. "I got lonely," he said.

"For me? Come on! We went years without seeing each other."

"For the city. The neighborhood."

"The action?"

"Yeah, there's that. Where I'm staying is like being in witness protection. There's nothing going on."

"Except being alive. You come back here and you're dead. Here's what's happening. You're going to walk. A deal is just about in place."

"You're shitting me!"

"No. It's almost done, but until it is, you've got a target on your back."

"You mean the money I owe Barak is forgiven?"

"That's the way it looks. But I suspect what Barak's going to want in return is your permanent absence from his, shall we say, sphere of influence."

"Why?"

"Because you would be a reminder of a promise not kept."

"You mean I could never come back here?" he said.

"The entire city."

He popped the tab on the can and took a long, slow drink.

"I don't know that I could do that."

"Oh, I think you can. You've got a double-edged sword here. If Barak doesn't frighten you enough, Dave should."

"What are you talking about?"

"Dave is brokering the arrangement."

"For me?"

"No, for me. Your former business partner planned to go after anyone who even knew you casually. I fit the bill. If it weren't for Dave, I'd be on a slab right now. Basically, Dave put himself on the line to keep me hale and hearty. You're a throw-in."

"I don't know what to say."

"How about good-bye, until I call and tell you everything's set?"

Danny studied the can as if trying to divine its mysteries. "What am I going to do?" he said. "Where am I going to go?"

I reached into my pocket, pulled out my money, and counted it. Just shy of two hundred dollars. I handed it to him.

"I'm going to call a cab," I said. "That should be enough to take you to where you're staying. Tomorrow, I'll go to the bank and withdraw a couple of thousand dollars. Consider it start-up money. You'll call me at noon and tell me where you want the wire sent."

He shook his head. "I can't do that," he said. "You know, take your money."

"Sure you can. It's not much, but that's all I can spare right now. And it's a gift, not a loan."

He pocketed the cash.

I went into the kitchen to call a cab. The dispatcher agreed to call me when the cab was out front. When I returned, I found Danny sitting with his head in his hands, rocking back and forth.

Suddenly there was a knock at the door. Danny stopped rocking. I walked into the bedroom, motioning him to follow. I reached under my bed and retrieved the Glock. I whispered to him to stay, and walked to the door and stood off to the side.

"Who is it?"

"Ginny."

It was turning into that kind of a day.

She noticed the Glock immediately. "I guess you weren't expecting me," she said.

The Mistress of Understatement.

"It's all right. Come on in."

She hesitated. "If this is a bad time . . ."

I pocketed the Glock. "Just winding up some business. Nothing to be concerned about."

Danny poked his head out of the bedroom. I waved him in.

"Danny?" Ginny said. "It's been years. What are you doing here?"

"Danny was just leaving."

"If I'm interrupting . . ."

"No, no," Danny said. "Steeg is right. I was just leaving."

As if on cue, the phone rang. It was the cab company.

I turned to Danny. "The cab's out front," I said. "Remember, call me tomorrow and tell me where you want the wire sent. OK?"

"I'll pay you back, Steeg. Every penny."

"Don't worry about it. You better go, the meter is running."

He said good-bye to Ginny, hugged me, and left.

"What was that all about?" she said.

"The wages of sin."

It occurred to me that Danny wasn't the only one the adage applied to.

"So, you're not going to tell me about it?" she said.

That she had just met her dead brother's business partner would only complicate things.

"Some things are better left unsaid. What brings you here?"

She thrust an envelope into my hands. "It's another one."

The next morning Dave stopped by. I told him Danny Reno had dropped in to say hello. He nearly went nuts.

"Your fucking buddy Reno is wearing me out," he said.

"Jesus taught us to care for the least among us."

"And look what it got Him. Reno is a fucking moron who, if he keeps this shit up, may not be among us much longer. And you're no better. I can't believe you gave him money."

"He's tapped. What was I supposed to do?"

"I don't believe that for a minute."

"You had to see him. He looks like a bag lady."

"Really! Remember Joey the Bum? Had this palsy thing going on? Used to panhandle on Broadway?"

"Sure. I used to slip him a few dollars now and then."

"Very generous. I'm sure he has a plaque in the lobby of one of the several buildings he owns dedicated to you."

"What do you mean?"

"He was clearing maybe three, four hundred a day. Cash. Take-home. No taxes. On matinee days he would do even better."

"How do you know?"

"I put Joey's money on the street. He made another four hundred in vig alone. Hand to God. When the palsy routine got old, he switched the act to a Vietnam veteran with AIDS. Used to sit in front of the theaters with a handwritten sign. He'd be there when they came in, when they broke after the first act, and when the show was over. Worked maybe three hours a day. Now he's retired to a condo in Boca. And you gave him money. Jesus Christ! You've got to be a changeling."

"That's what Pop always thought."

His face went dark.

"Fuck Dominic," Dave said. "If it wasn't for Norah, I would have killed him and taken pleasure in it."

"Just about every time we talk, the conversation somehow veers around to Dominic. He was a prick. He's dead. End of story. You've got to let it go."

"When they plant me in the ground."

"Let's get back to Joey the Bum. What's his connection to Danny?"

"They made their living the same way. Joey took care of business. So did Reno. He has money socked away. Count on it."

It was time to change the subject. "When are you meeting with Barak?"

"I have a call in to him. It'll be soon, though. So listen, I'm here for a reason."

"Besides making me feel stupid?"

"Dinner the other night didn't work out so well, and I want to make up for it by taking you to lunch. For a change, let's do something other than Feeney's. I love Nick, but enough's enough."

"I don't have anything going."

"Good. There's a new restaurant in Chelsea, Purslane, just opened."

"Now they're naming restaurants after weeds? Perfect."

"Who gives a shit? The food is supposed to be good. If that doesn't make you happy, I got another piece of bad news for you. Terry Sloan is joining us. He's building a house in the Hamptons and wants to show me the plans."

"The Hamptons? Did the city council vote itself a pay raise?"

"Terry always has an eye on opportunities."

"I'll take a rain check," I said.

"No, you won't. I know you don't like him, probably with good reason. But, like you, he's a fact of life, and I've gotta deal with him. The way I see it, if I gotta put up with Reno, you can put up with Sloan for a couple of hours. It's like you said about Dominic. Put it behind you, and move on."

Hard to argue with.

Purslane confirmed my worst suspicions. The restaurant was a celebration of weeds. They decorated the plates, appeared in watercolors on the walls, illuminated the margins of the menus, and served as the motif for the silverware. The menu offerings weren't much more promising. Everything was organic or artisanal, wildly overpriced, and as appetizing as hay. Couple that with Terry Sloan, sitting across from me and crowing about his new 15,000-square-foot house on the bay when he deserved to be in prison.

"So," Terry said, "they tell me it should be ready around the first of July, and it better be. I got this Fourth of July party planned. There's gonna be fireworks and an old-fashioned clambake. You know, the works. The invitations go out in a couple of weeks. Franny and the kids would love it."

I guess I didn't make the guest list. More's the pity.

"Just like the kind of party your constituents have on the Fourth," I said, "except for the clams and lobsters and mojitos part."

Dave threw me a look, but Terry continued, undaunted. "Hey, it's the country's birthday," he said.

Subtlety is one of the things that distinguishes humans from all other members of the animal kingdom. Terry failed to make the cut. "There's that," I agreed.

"Sounds great, Terry," Dave said. "If we can make it, we will."

"Terrific! Love to have you. You're invited too, Steeg."

Not only was Terry incapable of reading the shadings of language, he was a bust at reading Dave. My brother would rather have wild dogs play tug-of-war with his intestines than schlep out to the Hamptons on a holiday weekend. Dave's idea of a party was grilling some steaks for the family.

"Thanks, but I have a high colonic scheduled," I said.

Dave threw me another look, more menacing than the last.

"You gotta do what you gotta do," Terry said. "So, what do you think of the restaurant?"

"Nice place," Dave said.

I kept my mouth shut.

"Yeah," Terry said, "I've got a piece of it. A new business I'm into. We plan to open a bunch more."

That explained the Hamptons manse. "Really?" I said.

"Sure. The handwriting's on the wall. Healthy living is the future. No more smoking. No more trans fats. No more shit to clog up your arteries, no more—"

"Taste," I said.

"We get the point, Jake," Dave said. "Let's move on. OK?"

The waitress appeared, and Dave and Terry ordered drinks. I stuck with club soda with a lemon slice floating on top.

"I hear you had a thing with Pete Toal," Terry said.

"That's putting a fine point on it. I clocked him."

"Why?"

"He played me. Wasn't straight."

"What the hell does that mean?" he asked.

"I'd rather not go into it."

"You can't go around punching people in the mouth, Steeg," he said.

"Of course I can."

Terry turned to Dave. "You've gotta talk to him," he said.

"You're asking the wrong person," Dave said.

"Why do you care, Terry?" I said.

"You're pissing some people off."

Now we were getting to the heart of things. "You have my full attention. Who?"

"All I'm going to say is that Pete has some friends who don't like to see him smacked around."

"It's good to have faithful friends. But the thing I'm trying to figure out is whether it's the smacking around or something else that's bothering his pals. In other words, whose ox is being gored?"

"I don't understand."

"Oh," I said, "I think you do. With someone like Toal, there's always money involved. He could be hit by a bus and his *friends* wouldn't bother to send flowers. But screwing with the money flow might cause their concern."

"You're very distrustful, you know that, Jake?"

"It's the key to my longevity."

"Not if you keep going the way you're—"

Dave drove his salad fork into Terry's thigh.

"What the *fuck!*" Terry screamed.

Dave put his finger to Terry's lips. "Shhh! Don't make a scene."

A bunch of heads turned, and a waiter hurried over. Terry waved him off. The waiter glanced down, saw what was sticking out of Terry's thigh, and nearly puked.

With his hand still gripping the fork, Dave turned his attention to Terry. In a voice barely above a whisper he said, "You don't ever threaten my brother."

The color drained from Terry's face. "I . . . didn't . . . mean . . ." he gasped.

Dave dug the fork in deeper. "I don't give a shit. That's just the way it is. OK?"

Terry gagged, and nodded.

Dave yanked out the fork and dropped it on Terry's plate. Then he picked up the menu, looked at it briefly, and set it down.

"I think I'll have the trout. How about you, Jake?"

If anything, Dave was consistent. Blood was blood.

Terry didn't linger at the table—mumbled something about Bellevue's emergency room—and I had lost my appetite. But Dave didn't want to dine alone, so I stayed.

"You crossed the line with Terry," I said.

He laughed. "Whose line?"

"Mine," I said.

He wasn't laughing anymore. "He should have known better."

"I keep telling you, I'm tired of playing kid brother. I can take care of myself."

"The trout is good. Have some."

I've never figured out what makes Dave tick. Loving father and husband. Devoted brother. Stone killer. Capable of extraordinary acts of kindness, and mind-numbing cruelty. Dave was born with a port-wine stain on his cheek that caused him no end of grief. When he was with the Westies, a notorious West Side gang of Irish psycho murderers, one of the doped-up donkeys, a guy named Brian Grace, took special delight in fucking with Dave over the port-wine stain. Mickey Featherstone, the ringleader of the lunatic crew, ordered Dave to let it ride. And he did, for a very short while. One Christmas Eve, Grace was drinking at Feeney's. Dave showed up with an acetylene torch. Nick held Grace down while Dave went to work on his face. Afterwards, Grace was a chastened man, and Dave went home and set the presents under the tree.

The closest I've come to explaining my brother is that he's either a master compartmentalizer or a total fucking lunatic. How else to account for the bizarre dichotomy that gums up his moral compass? With Dave, true north is a shifting target.

It was something we never talked about, but the Terry Sloan incident, coupled with the kidnapping of Barak's son, gave me the feeling that Dave was about to crater.

"Couldn't you have made your point another way?"

"We're back on that? No. See, that's the only thing guys like Terry understand."

"What do you mean?"

"The day before their first Election Day, they're average schmucks. The day after, they're suddenly important, and everybody kisses their ass like it's the pope's ring. Why? Because they have something they never had before. Power. And they think they're invincible. And then they meet someone like me—or Barak—and get a glimpse of the real thing. The few smart ones understand reality right from the get-go. But guys like Terry require the occasional object lesson."

"So this wasn't a spur-of-the-moment thing," I said.

"It never is." He smiled and held out a forkful of trout. "You gotta try this. It really is good."

"But that doesn't make it right."

He put the fork down on his plate. "Do you remember Angelo Carpozzi?" he said.

"He was a cop."

"Right. A big ape of a guy. When I was younger, whenever he would run into me—at a restaurant, out on the street, wherever—he would take me into an alley, rip a button off his uniform, and play a riff on my skull with his nightstick. If I fought back or lodged a complaint—which I would never do—he could say I attacked him. Remember the ripped-off button? I don't know how many times the guinea bastard kicked the shit out of me."

"He was a bad cop and didn't deserve to wear the badge," I said.

"Or maybe he was just doing his job cleaning up the neighborhood."

"That's nuts."

"No, it's power. And sometimes you've got to break the rules for the greater good."

"What's the greater good in stabbing Terry?"

"He knows I'm not to be fucked with."

"You don't see the distinction, do you?" I said.

"What's the greater good with guys who never served in the military wrapping themselves in the flag and sending kids Anthony's age off to bring democracy to fucks who would rather kill each other? And when our guys come back with body parts missing, the same guys who sent them treat them like shit on the bottom of their shoes. Explain the morality of hiring a CEO and paying him millions a year, and then the geniuses who hired him throw even more money at him when they figure out he's a yutz and can his ass? Do you want me to go on?"

"I get the point."

"And it's about fucking time. Look, I understand where you're coming from, Jake. But understand me. All I give a fuck about is the well-being of my family. Everything else is nothing." He planted his arms on the table and leaned forward. "So, where does that leave us?"

"I'm not sure."

"Then you better figure it out."

I wasn't sure that I could.

Dave offered me a lift. I needed to walk.

It was an unusually balmy day, and the streets were clogged. After a few blocks, I stopped to check my messages. There was one. Stuart's accountants had come through. I headed over to Été.

Stuart was one of those people who look overwhelmed even when they are sleeping. Short, abrupt movements. Hurried speech. Mind always somewhere else.

"Good to see you again," I said. "What do you have for me?"

He handed me a thick manila envelope. "All the charge receipts and cash transactions for that evening. The originals. I would have made copies, but I just didn't have the time."

I slipped the envelope under my arm. "Can I take them with me?"

He shook his head. "Uh-uh. But you can use my new office. Actually, it's Noonan's old office. I've got his job now. Probationary. Seems like they're trying me out."

"Good for you, Stuart."

He blushed. "It wasn't the way I wanted to get it, but . . ."

"You'll take it."

"I guess. Come on, I'll show you where it is."

I followed him through the dining room and into the back. We stopped at what looked like a broom closet with a desk jammed into it.

"Everything you need is right here," he said. "If you need to make copies, the machine is in the corner. I've got to get back. There's so much to do. One thing after another. I'll be out front if you need me."

"Appreciate it, Stuart."

I opened the envelope and spread its contents on the desk. The accountants had made my job easy. There were two packets secured by rubber bands. One contained charge receipts. The other, much smaller packet contained cash receipts. Included also was a spreadsheet listing each transaction, cash or charge, by time and amount. Operating on the "trust no one" theory, I added the charge receipts and checked the total against the spreadsheet. It tallied. Not surprising. It's nearly impossible to fudge charges. Then I went back through the charge receipts and looked for Ferris's name.

No dice.

That meant he either paid cash or someone else paid the bill. I rechecked the charge receipts, searching for any familiar name, and came up with nothing. I guess I didn't travel in those rarefied circles.

Next, I turned my attention to the cash receipts. They came to eight thousand dollars. The spreadsheet showed six. Someone had his hand in the till. The IRS gets the spreadsheet, and the receipts get lost. Not surprising, but it still didn't answer the question of whether Ferris was at the restaurant the night he was murdered.

And then it hit me, something Toal had said about the ME's report. I went looking for Stuart.

I found him at the reservations desk and handed him the receipts.

"Find what you were looking for?" he asked.

Raising the possibility of skimming with Stuart wasn't a good idea. For all I knew, he could be the skimmer, but I doubted it. But my guts insisted that skimming was a piece of the puzzle, and I knew just the guy who could help me get to the bottom of it.

"I think so."

"Glad to help," he said. "By the way, if you're in the neighborhood some evening, I'd love for you to be my guest for dinner."

"I might just do that. Thanks."

He handed me a menu. On the way out I looked at it.

And I had the answer.

Kenny stood with his back against the bar, sipping from a bottle of water. I had called him and asked him to meet me at Feeney's. He didn't look happy to see me, and I didn't blame him. Our relationship thus far wasn't what he bargained for. And it wasn't about to improve.

"Are you hungry?" I asked.

"Always."

"How about a kosher meal? My treat."

His eyes narrowed. "What're you setting me up for?"

"Not a thing. Just two friends enjoying a meal. I'll even spring for the cab."

"You mean it?"

"Not exactly."

"That's what I thought," he said.

He took me to a restaurant in the Forties, west of Madison. We both ordered the rib eye steaks, on the bone. It was great.

"What makes food kosher?" I asked. "Like, why can't you eat pork? I always figured it had something to do with trichinosis, or that pigs rolled around in crap."

"Nothing to do with it. It's because God said so. He's very clear about what's permissible and what isn't, and that's it."

"Really? What about mixing milk and meat?"

"More complicated, but pretty much the same thing."

"Fascinating."

"Look, I'd love to discuss this with you further, but what shit job do you have lined up for me?"

"What makes you think it's a shit job?"

"I'm a fast learner," he said.

"Can you get me the names of the owners of a particular restaurant?"

"Sure. But it's probably a corporation."

"Can you pierce the veil?"

"With a little work. What's the restaurant?"

"Été."

"That place across from where those guys tried to kill you."

"That's the one."

"It will be my pleasure," Kenny said. "Anything else?"

"I don't think so."

"Why do I feel like the governor just pardoned me?"

"I seem to have that effect on people."

"I actually enjoy working with you," Kenny said.

"That truly is a mystery."

"No, I'm serious. Stuff seems to happen to you, and that makes things fun."

"It occurred to me I know very little about you, Kenny. Are you married?"

"I was. Nice lady. She couldn't put up with my life. I couldn't blame her."

"Any kids?"

"Two. Six and four. She won't let me see them. Says it isn't good for them to have somebody like me in their lives."

"I'm very sorry."

He shrugged. "You make choices, and you have to live with them. I do see them, though. She doesn't know it, but I see them. I know their schedules to the minute. When they go to the park. When they go to school. They don't know I'm there, but I see them. Beautiful kids. Getting bigger every day."

"I didn't mean to open this can of worms."

"It's not a can of worms," he said. "It's my life. And what about you, Steeg?"

"What about me?"

"What's important to you?"

"The people I love. Family."

"So, maybe we're not too different."

Could be Dave had it right after all.

needed some alone time.

My lungs burned, I was bone tired and in no mood for company. What I was looking forward to was a quiet evening at home. Catch up on some reading. Listen to some music. And turn in early. As much as I hated to admit it, I was wearing down, and coming to grips with my own fragility was something I wasn't used to. I had been grappling with Ferris's murder and the Danny Reno situation for a while. My bread had been cast out on the waters, and I wanted to sit back and let the tide bring something in.

I popped a Carter Family CD into the CD player, opened the newspaper to the sports section, and stretched out on the sofa. Fifteen minutes later my doorbell rang. I seriously considered not answering. I should have gone with my instincts. I hauled my body up and went to the door.

The tide hadn't been kind. Jeanmarie and Ollie stood at my threshold.

"Can we come in?" she asked.

"This is not a good time."

"Do you have company?"

"No."

"Then it's a good time," she said.

She brushed past me. Ollie trailed in her wake.

By the time I closed the door and got back to the living room, she and Ollie had settled in on the sofa.

Hoping to send the message that this would be a short visit, I stood.

"What do you want?" I said.

She reached over and plucked a vase from an end table. "Remember this, Ollie?" she said. "We gave it to Ginny on their first anniversary."

Her tone implied that I had somehow stolen the vase.

"Take it, it's yours."

She replaced the vase.

"It wasn't expensive anyway," she said.

Jeanmarie was in rare form.

"Why are you here?"

She looked around the living room. "How do you do it, Steeg?"

"Do what?"

"Live alone. Your mother, Norah, always said you didn't need anybody. Said that you'd be perfectly happy sitting on a stump in the middle of a field with only yourself for company. Didn't she say that, Ollie?"

Ollie appeared to have something else on his mind.

"It's a wise mother who knows her own children, Jeanmarie," I said.

"Are you saying I don't know my children?"

"I'm saying that I'm not up to dealing with you tonight. What's on your mind?"

"Tell him, Ollie."

But Ollie didn't seem to be in the mood for idle talk. He looked away and rubbed his hands together as if trying to warm them.

"Let's go home, Jeanmarie, and leave him be. The lad looks poorly."

"He always looks like this. *Tell him*, I said."

I wondered what sin Ollie had committed in some previous incarnation to wind up with someone like Jeanmarie.

"Tell me what, Ollie?"

"I screwed up, Steeg. Got caught up in something and it's coming back on my family."

"What are you talking about?"

He looked down at his hands and then at Jeanmarie, who stared straight ahead, stone-faced. Realizing there was no help there, he continued.

"I was there that night. Outside of the gay bar. I saw what they did to that boy, and I ran."

"You were at Neon?"

"Aye. I saw you come in. Surprised me. Never figured you for one of those."

I didn't know whether to laugh or cry. The man was beyond redemption.

"Why were you there?"

"Went out to hoist a few with Liam's friends. Hit a few bars, everyone was feeling good. It was getting late and I wanted to pack it in, and the fella they call Big Tiny wouldn't hear of it. His blood was truly up that night. Said the fun was just starting. And that's how we wound up there."

"And you and the other assholes beat that man to death?"

"No, I had no part of it. The Nancy boy was up the corner from the bar. Looked to be waiting for someone. The boys went up to him. Pushed him around a bit. Told him they wanted him to . . . do things to them. He was so scared I thought he would piss himself. He tried to get away, but . . . you know the rest. They were on him like a pack of wolves. Never figured it would come to that."

"Why would you get involved with these people, Ollie?"

"Because," Jeanmarie spat, "the man's a layabout, not a proper man, a slug who can't hold a job for three days in a row and blames everyone else for his shortcomings. If it's not the blacks, it's the Jews, or the Puerto Ricans. Always someone else. May as well be the Martians. Ah, what's the use! He is what he is, and I'm stuck with him."

"Now, Jeanmarie . . ." Ollie said.

She cut him off. "Don't you 'Jeanmarie' me. You tell Steeg everything, or I'll put you out of the house."

He looked down at his hands again, his voice barely above a whisper. "It was me who sent Tony those letters."

The Universe had finally kicked in.

"Why?"

"He was a nigger, and my daughter brought disgrace on our family when she married him."

"*You* disgrace this family," Jeanmarie said.

"Where did you get this from?"

"Stuff Liam brought home. Pamphlets and such."

"Like father, like son. Not a brain between them. Wonderful family I raised."

"And you believe this twisted shit?" I said.

Ollie looked away.

"I did, God forgive me," he said.

Some things just take your breath away.

I looked at Jeanmarie.

"Do you buy this crap too?" I said.

"I believe in the Holy Mother Church and its teachings. I also know that Ollie is going to burn throughout eternity for his sins. But he didn't kill Tony, and while he's here on earth, I will not allow my husband to be punished for something he did not do."

I turned back to Ollie. "Tell me about Ferris."

"I wrote him notes. Telephoned him. Warned him what would happen if he didn't leave my daughter."

"And?"

The room was very still.

"Wanted him dead," he said. "I followed him, looking for the right opportunity."

"And you had a few but never followed through."

He looked down at his hands. "Aye," he said.

"How about the night he was murdered?"

"Jeanmarie and I were at church. Most Precious Blood."

Now, *that* was an alibi!

"Why are you telling me this now?"

"I'm worried for my daughter," Ollie said. "I've put her in danger."

"Ginny mentioned she received a note after Ferris was killed, and I couldn't figure out why. But I have a feeling you're going to solve that little mystery."

"Aye, Tiny knows I wasn't happy about killing that lad at the bar. He's afraid I won't keep my mouth shut. So now the bastard's using Ginny to keep me quiet."

"I didn't know Ollie was behind these things when I first asked for your help, Steeg," Jeanmarie said. "Appears that I need your help again."

I think there was a compliment buried somewhere in there.

"It's already been taken care of," I said.

"What do you mean?"

"Trust me, Big Tiny's writing days are over. What now, Ollie?"

"My conscience is clean," he said.

"Really!"

"That night at church, I made my first confession in I don't know how many years. Father Burke said that for my sins to be forgiven I had to make a clean breast of things. That's why I'm here."

"Have you told Ginny?"

"I have. And she's done with me. I don't blame her. Tony dead. Liam too. Colleen, living Lord knows what kind of life. And it's my fault. I was a piss-poor father to my children."

Ollie was back to feeling sorry for himself, and it made me want to puke.

"That you were, and a piss-poor imitation of a man. But if it's sympathy you're looking for, I'm fresh out. Maybe a few more Acts of Contrition will do the trick."

That men like Ollie exist is a hell of a comment on the human condition, and an enduring wonder. At Most Precious Blood, we were taught that God gave us a "one size fits all" path to Him. The problem is, guys like Ollie develop their own twisted theologies to fit God. The things we do in His name truly chill the soul.

I called Luce.

"You're not going to believe this one," I said.

"Wanna bet?"

I filled her in on the latest twist.

"Where in hell did he come up with this stuff?"

"Christian Identity horseshit."

"Are these the folks who live in Idaho and see black helicopters in their dreams?"

"The very same. Skinheads. Klansmen. Posse Comitatus. Neo-Nazis. The truly fucked up who live among us."

"Does he realize these miscreants are not too thrilled with Catholics, either?"

"You're expecting a moron to be rational? Come on!"

"How in hell did he get involved with this stuff?"

"Ollie works intermittently, so he has a lot of time on his hands."

"Do you believe that he didn't kill Ferris?"

"Yeah. But it adds a whole new dimension to my theory of the case."

"Which was?"

"I didn't actually have one till now, but it's beginning to take shape."

"Care to share?"

"Not quite yet. You'll only shoot it full of holes."

"Why do I get the feeling that you flunked 'Plays Well with Others' at school? What else is going on?"

"Still haven't heard from Banas, the missing Été waiter," I said.

"I'm surprised. I thought the job interview bit would work like a charm."

"So did I. Want to go back up to the Bronx and try again?"

"I shudder at the thought," she said. "Let's give him one more day."

"I tell you, Luce, the longer I live, the less things surprise me."

"If you keep the bar low, you'll never be disappointed. What else is going on?"

"I'm convinced that Ferris did indeed have his last meal at Été, and he either paid cash or his companion—and possible killer—picked up the tab."

" 'Convinced' is a strong word," she said.

"It was something Toal said. A detail from the ME's report. The official cause of death was blunt-force trauma to the back of the head. Toal said he might have been hit with a wrench."

"And they never recovered the murder weapon," Luce said.

"Right. And then Toal threw something else into the mix that I had completely forgotten about."

"It happens."

"Unfortunately. Anyway, it had to do with Ferris's stomach contents. His last meal was an endive and radicchio salad."

"Sounds like Ferris was trying to watch his weight," she said. "Poor bastard picked the wrong time for it."

"I asked Stuart, the manager at Été, if that salad was on the menu."

"And he said it was."

"Been there since the restaurant opened."

"So, it's a pretty good inference that he was there. I'm proud of you, Jackson. Any idea who he was with?"

"That's where our amazing disappearing waiter comes in. All I know is, Ferris didn't charge the meal."

"Which means he paid cash, or his killer charged it."

"Assuming that his dinner partner killed him."

"And you're not there yet."

"Uh-uh. Every time I think I'm on to something promising, it takes me in a new direction."

"Ain't cop work fun?"

The next morning my chest felt like a nagging toothache. I called the doc and described the symptoms. He was surprised. Said I had been healing nicely. Asked if I had been under any stress lately. Some, I admitted. He asked a few more questions, probing a little deeper, then pronounced me an asshole, and refused to see me. Said he would rather spend time with more intelligent patients. Hard to argue with. I dragged myself out of bed and went to Feeney's for breakfast.

Nick looked worse than I felt. "I've got a problem," he said.

"I'm fresh out of solutions. Have your guys come up with Lisa Hernandez's new address yet?"

"They're working on it. Don't worry. Can we get back to my problem now?"

"Make it easy, please."

"Noreen is leaving me. Five years of marriage down the tubes. Can you believe it?"

"I'm surprised she married you in the first place. She's number two, right?"

"Number three, and thanks for being sympathetic."

"You're right, I apologize. I know you were deeply in love and it must hurt, but broken hearts mend, and you'll come out of this a stronger man. How's that?"

"You're an asshole, you know that?"

I guess that made it unanimous.

"Nick, you know I love you like a brother, but your kids have had three different moms in their lives, and you've been cheating on Noreen since the day you married her."

"Actually, before I married her."

"Then what's the problem?"

"Now Marie, my girlfriend, wants to get married, and I don't think I can handle it."

"Then tell her no."

"Marie knows where the money is."

"How did that happen?"

"She's my accountant. Helped me hide it from Noreen."

"Are you and Marie planning a big wedding?"

He ran his fingers through his hair. "I'm screwed, ain't I?" he said.

"Royally."

He got up from the table and pushed the chair in. "I got to figure this thing out," he said.

Just then Pete Toal walked in. The day was heading into the dumper.

"Mind if I sit?" he said.

"Would it matter?"

"You do make it tough, don't you?"

"What's on your mind, Pete?"

"I'm here to square things, make things right between us. I was out of line, and if I were in your shoes, I would've done the same thing."

Contrition fit Toal like a bad suit. I had a sneaking suspicion the fine hand of Terry Sloan was at work here.

"This wasn't your idea, was it?" I said.

"What are you driving at?"

"How's Terry doing? Healing nicely, I trust."

Toal's fingers beat a tattoo on the tabletop. "What do you want, Steeg."

"Some answers."

"Depends on the question," he said.

"Fair enough. What's Terry's interest in you?"

"We go back a long way. Y'know, friends."

"Are you on his pad?"

"Everyone's on some kind of a pad."

"What is that supposed to mean?"

"You call it a pad, I call it friends doing favors for friends. In a manner of speaking, you're on a pad too."

"Whose is that?"

"Dave's. He does what he does, and you look the other way. Even when you wore the badge. In return, he looks out for you. Tell me I'm wrong."

I couldn't. It was another in a long list of moral dilemmas I was trying to work out.

"It's a bit more complicated than that," I said.

"Always is."

"The difference is, I never ask for his help."

"May be. But you still live in his halo. He's there whether you want him or not."

"Why weren't you straight with me about the Ferris investigation?"

"I thought I was."

"You left some things out. Why?"

"I gave you what you asked for," he said.

"Not all of it."

He shrugged.

"How does Terry profit from his relationship with you?" I asked.

He shook his head and threw me a pitying look. "You never stop pushing, do you, Steeg?"

"It's what keeps my juices flowing."

"Remember Icarus? Dumb fuck didn't listen, and look what happened. Crashed and burned when he flew too close to the sun."

Toal got to his feet and patted me on the shoulder. "See you around, Steeg," he said.

The fence mending with Allie was starting to pick up steam. We had dinner that evening and wound up at her apartment.

"I think I'm going to renew my membership at the gym," Allie said, emerging from the shower completely wrapped in an oversize green bath towel. A smaller yellow towel was wrapped turbanlike around her head. She looked like a tall daffodil.

"Why is that?" I said.

"Sex is over for us."

This wasn't the postcoital remark I was longing to hear. Something more in the way of "Gee, you were great," or "Where have you been all my life, sailor?" would have been far more esteem enhancing. I sat up in her bed and adjusted some puffy pillows behind my head. I loved those puffy pillows.

"I thought it was wondrous, and from those barely re-strained shrieking sounds you made, I sensed that you felt that way too."

She slid into bed and nestled her body against mine. She smelled of lilacs and candy apples. "I did," she said. "And therein lies the problem."

This was bewildering. "What problem?"

"It was so good that I worry about consistency," she said.

"Consistency?"

She moved her damp terry-cloth-covered body closer and stroked my toes with hers. "What if there's a drop-off?"

"A drop-off?" I was reduced to repeating everything she said as a question.

"Look, we've set ourselves up for disappointment," she said.

I restrained myself from repeating the word *disappointment* as a question.

She continued. "We've set the bar too high. Sex can't always be this good. It's not *normal*! Ergo, it's inevitable that there's going to be a drop-off. Then you'll blame me, and I'll blame you, then we'll blame ourselves, and wind up hating each other."

"That's a lot of blame to go around," I said.

"And that's not all."

"There's more?"

"Sure. We're going to turn into those people you see in Hopper paintings."

"We will?"

"Exactly. Two people occupying the same space but never connecting, and doomed to spend the rest of their lives in sterile emptiness."

"And you think about this."

"Every waking moment."

"Which brings us to . . ."

She completed my sentence: "Consistency."

"Emerson said a foolish consistency is the hobgoblin of little minds."

"But he doesn't share my bed," she said.

"There isn't room. Don't you think you should trade up to at least a queen?"

She wriggled a leg out from under her terry cocoon and slung it over mine and flashed me a devilish grin.

"I could, but it wouldn't be as much fun," she said.

"How's life in the ad game?"

"If it weren't for the people, it would be great."

"I can see how that would be a problem," I said.

"You don't know the half of it. It's a vast conspiracy of idiots. How's your sleuthing going?"

"Shifting into high gear. I now know who didn't murder Ginny's husband."

She looked puzzled. "And that's a good thing?"

"A very good thing."

"Because it narrows down your list of suspects?"

"It would, if I had suspects. Right now all I have are suspicions."

"And that makes you happy."

"Positively joyous."

With a move that was startlingly swift, she wound up on top of me. The upper half of her body was propped up on her arms, enveloping us both in damp green terry cloth. Her body moved against mine.

"How much longer are we going to talk?" she said.

"Apparently not much. What did you have in mind?"

"Testing the consistency theory."

"Could you do that astonishing thing you did before?"

"If you play your cards right."

And she did.

It was consistent.

Now all I had to do was keep it that way.

The next morning I was in Dave's car on our way to meet with Barak. Sitting in the backseat, between two of Dave's men, was Barak's son, Ari.

"Why am I here, Dave?"

"Barak requested your presence. Apparently he trusts you."

"Where are you doing the handoff?"

"Sheepshead Bay. Out in the open. Where the fishing boats dock."

"Wise choice."

We drove along the Belt Parkway, passing under the Verrazano-Narrows Bridge—New York's version of the St. Louis Gateway Arch—and followed the coastline.

"You sure do get mixed up with crazies, Jake, my boy. First Reno, then Liam and his skinhead buddies. Now, that's a parlay. What is it with you?"

"Maybe they see a kindred spirit," I said.

We passed Coney Island. The reddish-orange Parachute Jump jutted into the sky like a postmodern art installation.

"And then there's Ollie, the Nazi with an AARP card in his wallet."

"You can't make it up," I said.

"That whole fucking family is off the rails. Where does Ginny fit in all this?"

"Now, that's a really good question."

"You think she married Ferris to get back at Ollie?"

"Could be. She probably married me to get back at Jeanmarie."

"And people think the Steegs are screwed up," he said.

"We're not?"

We took the Knapp Street exit, took a right, and then another right at Emmons Avenue. The piers were up ahead. And so was Barak. Alone.

We pulled into a parking spot. One of Dave's men got out of the car, motioning for Ari to follow. I expected him to run to his father. Instead, with quiet dignity, he slowly walked toward him. Talk about the apple not falling far from the tree! Barak kissed the top of his head and draped his arm on Ari's shoulder.

Dave and I got out of the car. He walked up to Barak.

"So, we're done here, right?" Dave said. "I kept my word."

He ignored Dave. Instead, he said to me, "It's good to see you again, Mr. Steeg."

I nodded.

"Your friend Reno. Is he well?"

"He is."

"And he understands the terms of our agreement?"

"He does."

"And you? Are you well, Mr. Steeg?"

"I am."

"Do you remember what I promised you the last time we met?"

For every tear my son has shed, there will be a reckoning. It was something I would never forget.

"I do. But as you can see, he's fine."

"I will be the judge of that," he said.

It was Dave's party, and he didn't appreciate being left out. "It's over, then," he said.

Barak's face was stone. He took his son's hand and said, "Thank you for returning my boy."

And then he and his son walked off.

"That's one cold son of a bitch," Dave said. "But at least that's one less thing to worry about."

I wondered when the other shoe would drop.

■

When we got back to Feeney's, Dave was in an expansive mood. Clapping people on the back. Buying drinks for the rummies. Having a high old time.

"So, Jakey," he said, putting me in a headlock, "your brother pulled it off. Stared down the Golem and made him blink first. You're off the hook, and you can tell Reno that he gets to live a little longer."

"Looks that way."

"Hey, Nick, look at this mope. Come on, Jake. Lighten up. This is a good thing."

I pasted on a smile. "You're right, it's a good thing."

"OK," Dave said. "Everything is back to normal."

I wasn't too sure of that.

"You and Barak seemed kind of cozy back there."

"Like you said, he trusts me."

"He said something to you. What was he talking about?"

"Nothing."

The door opened, and one of Barak's men strolled in. I remembered him from my meeting with Barak outside of Lisa Hernandez's building.

He scanned the room until his eyes fell on me. He wasn't smiling.

"Mr. Steeg, I have something for you."

He pulled an envelope from his jacket pocket and handed it to me. My name was printed on it. Then he left.

I opened it and found a tissue inside. It was damp.

"What is this, some kind of joke?" Dave said. "Who is this guy?"

"One of Barak's gun dogs."

"What did he want?"

I told him.

Dave appeared to take Barak's threat in stride, but I knew better. Behind the lopsided grin and the comments about how much fun this would be, there was real concern. For me, the forced bonhomie wore thin. To quote one of Luce's favorite expressions, I felt like a possum had just trotted over my grave. I had no idea what it meant, but it certainly wasn't anything good.

Thinking of Luce reminded me that I still hadn't heard from Banas. It didn't make sense. He was a waiter who needed a job. He should've jumped at my letter. I started to worry that the same person who had done Noonan had cleaned up the rest of the loose ends, including Banas. I hopped a train to the Bronx.

This time his roommate answered the door, and I learned what had befallen the estimable Roberto Banas. I called Luce and asked her to meet me at the Q101R bus stop in Queensboro Plaza.

■

Housing about fifteen thousand inmates in ten jails, Rikers Island is New York City's largest prison. A 415-acre City of Jails.

The only way in is a bus ride from Queens over the Francis Buono Bridge.

"I can't believe Banas is in the system," Luce said. "What in hell did he do?"

"According to his roommate, when he got canned, he started drinking, and he got picked up on a drunk and disorderly. The guy has family in Mexico who he's supporting, and all of a sudden the money dries up, so he went on a bender."

"Why didn't he get another job?"

"He's illegal, and that's in the news right now. Prospective employers are jittery. But Banas had another problem. The deceased Mr. Noonan wouldn't give him a reference."

"What a sweetie," Luce said. "No wonder Noonan is no longer with us. Are they looking at Banas for Noonan's murder?"

"He was in Rikers at the time. I'm surprised the feds haven't snatched him and sent him back to Mexico."

"They have other things on their mind right now," Luce said.

"That they do."

The bus came to a stop at the George Motchan Detention Center, and we got off.

"It's time to work your magic with your little gold badge," I said.

"So that's why you called. And here I was thinking you loved me for who I am."

"It's a little bit of both."

Luce's badge worked like a charm. She told the corrections officer at the reception desk that we wanted to see Roberto Banas, and from there it was open sesame. We went through security and were passed on to another guard, who led us to an interview room.

There's nothing to compare with the experience of being in a jail, the pervasive sullenness that exists on both sides of the bars. Combine that with the incessant battering of noise, and the sour odor of unwashed bodies, and you have a pretty good approximation of hell.

After a few minutes, Banas was ushered in. Luce told the CO we wanted to speak to Banas alone. No problem, he said, and left.

Banas was slight and dark-skinned, and wearing the clothes he had been arrested in. His eyes had the weary look of resignation.

"Mr. Banas, my name is Steeg, and this is my partner, Luce Guidry. Please take a seat."

A table separated us. Banas pulled up a chair and leaned back.

"You Immigration?" he said. "I wondered when you'd finally show up."

Luce showed him her badge.

"NYPD. We're not interested in your legal status, Mr. Banas," she said. "We're investigating a murder."

Now there was panic in his eyes.

"*Madre de Dios!* I was in a bar, and some guy took a swing at me. The next thing I know, I'm being booked. I never had trouble with the police before. You can check it out. Now you're talking murder?"

"Relax, Mr. Banas, we're not accusing you of killing anyone."

"Then what is it?"

"How long did you work at Été?" I said.

"Since it opened. About six months. And then the bastard Noonan fired me."

"Noonan is dead."

"So that's what this is about?"

"No. I want you to think back to about a month or so ago. A body was found in the restaurant alley."

"I remember. Everybody was talking about it."

I slid Ferris's picture across the table.

"Do you recognize him?"

He studied the picture. "Is that the guy who was killed?"

"It is."

"You think I waited on him?"

"I don't know. That's what I'm asking."

"I don't know. Could be. But . . ."

He put the picture down. This was going nowhere.

"He may have paid with cash," I said.

Banas picked the picture up again and grew excited. "Wait a minute!" he said. "Yeah, that's the guy. Paid with three one-hundred-dollar bills. Crisp. Just laid them on the table. When I picked them up, he was gone. Just left the money on the table. Didn't even give him a bill. Yeah, I remember him."

"Was he with anybody?"

"It's been a while, but I think so. A woman, maybe."

"Do you remember what she looked like? Try really hard."

Banas stared at the picture, and then at the ceiling.

"It was busy that night. I remember there was a birthday party at the next table. It was crazy. They were drinking, and singing at the top of their lungs. Then one of the women jumps up, and she wants me to take pictures, then she rubs herself all over me. Her I remember. Blonde. Real tall. Hot. You know."

"I'm happy for you, but how about the other woman?"

"I know she was there, but . . . Tell me what you want me to say and I'll say it."

"That's OK, Mr. Banas," Luce said. "You've been a great help."

"Look, I'm serious. I gotta get out of here. You don't know what it's like. These guys are fucking crazy."

"Do you have a lawyer?" I asked.

His face screwed up in distate. "Sure," he said. "Legal Aid. I speak better English than he does."

"Have you been arraigned yet?"

"Yeah, but I can't make the bond. And I got Immigration to worry about. I'm screwed."

I threw Luce a "We've got to help this guy" look. She picked up on the cue.

"What's your lawyer's name, Mr. Banas?"

"Somoza. Richard Somoza."

"And the DA?"

"I don't know. Some woman. Somoza should have it."

"I'll see what I can do."

"I appreciate it. Just don't let them send me back."

"When you get out, your old job should be waiting for you."

"Are you serious?"

"I'll speak to Stuart," I said. "I think I can persuade him."

Banas looked like he was about to cry. "You do that, and I swear to God I'll never take a drink again."

That used to be my line.

The Universe was in overdrive.

The pool of potential witnesses—or killers—had been whittled down to two. Now the trick was to get it down to one. I called Ginny and asked her to meet me at the Terminal Diner on Twelfth Avenue.

Her face was pale and drawn. No hint of makeup. "I understand you spoke to Ollie," she said.

"He and Jeanmarie stopped by."

"Some family, huh?"

"Some family," I agreed.

"I'm thankful for one thing, though."

"What's that?"

"We never had any kids. It's one thing for me to swim around in their polluted gene pool. It's quite another to invite my children in for a dip."

"You can't be surprised. Ollie was always a hater."

"Yeah, but no more so than most people in the Kitchen. I never would've thought he'd take it so far."

"I heard the same crap you did growing up, but it was just talk."

"You think? Back in high school I had a girlfriend who dated a black guy. She had an attitude and was going to show everyone. She showed them all right."

"What happened?"

"Some of the boys got together and told her they didn't want him coming around anymore. She told them to piss off. No one was going to tell her who she could date. He came around again. They threw him off a roof. When she went to his funeral, her parents put her out. Lovely."

"Jesus!"

"You know what was worse? The cops did nothing. They knew who did it, and they buried it."

"There have always been jerkoffs like that on the police force. Eventually, they get weeded out."

It sounded lame, but it was largely true.

"Do they, now! The particular jerkoff who caught the case managed to retire and live out his life on a pension. In case you're interested, his name was Dominic Steeg. So do me a favor, Jake. Don't tell me it was all just talk."

That was another entry in Dominic's ledger. One more thing to deal with in purgatory.

"Let's make a deal," I said. "I won't ask you to apologize for Ollie, and I won't apologize for Dominic."

She extended her hand, pinkie out, across the table. I did the same with mine.

"Pinkie swear," she said.

I gripped her pinky in mine. "Pinkie swear."

We touched our fingers to our lips.

"You know, when I found out what Ollie did, I wanted to kill him."

"Why didn't you?"

She shrugged.

"OK," she said, "what's so important?"

"It's something we covered before, but we're going to go over it again."

"Don't you trust me, Jake?"

"So far, you haven't given me a reason not to."

The expression on her face said it wasn't the answer she was looking for.

"On the night he was murdered, Tony had dinner with a woman. Surprised?"

"Not really. As I explained to you, we had an . . . *unconventional* marriage. Tony did his thing, and I did mine."

"Any idea who he was with?"

"We never discussed our . . . you know. It would have taken the fun out of things."

"Fun?"

"Sure. The sneaking around. The risk of getting caught. It's a turn-on."

"And that night you were having *fun* in your bedroom in Seaside."

"Save the sarcasm for someone who gives a crap. That's where I was."

"I'm going to have to talk to your boyfriend."

"Fine. I know I'm asking a lot, but be discreet. His wife doesn't know about us, and he has young children. Don't screw it up for him."

"As Dave is wont to say, 'You pay your money, you take

your chances.' To quote you, 'Part of the fun is taking risks.' But there's always a downside."

"Look, Tony and I indulged each other's fantasies. We were adults. It was innocent, and no one got hurt."

Except Tony.

S ir Walter Scott was right on the money. It's a hell of a tangled web we weave, when first we practice to deceive, and it was hard keeping all the deceivers straight. But buried somewhere inside was the one string that, when gently tugged, would cause the whole thing to unravel. All I had to do was find it. The prospect made my head hurt.

I went to Feeney's to see how Nick's guys were progressing in their hunt for the elusive Lisa Hernandez. Before I had the chance to ask, he produced her new address.

"And here you were thinking Nick's not gonna come through," he said.

"The thought had crossed my mind. Where is it?"

"Dobbs Ferry. Up in Westchester."

"Very bucolic."

"Whatever. You want company?"

"You haven't left this place in years. Why the sudden wanderlust?"

"More women problems. My soon-to-be ex-wife set her lawyers on me, and my wannabe next wife is a crazy lady. I gotta get away for a while. Do you want company, or what? I'll even drive."

Hard to refuse.

The drive up the Saw Mill River Parkway was just what I needed; the trees had just begun to leaf out, and between them vines had massed to produce soft mounds of green.

"So," I said, "what are you going to do about your marital problems?"

"Stop listening to my dick."

"Seems like a plan."

"Tell me about it. If I had gone into the priesthood like my mother wanted, I wouldn't be in this position."

"We all ultimately disappoint our parents."

"Ain't it the truth. Being a priest is a pretty good gig, though. They get a salary, free room and board, and if they play their cards right, they can make cardinal one day. Shit, then you're talking big money."

"I never looked at it that way. But the downside is there's no sex."

"We both know that's not exactly true. I got a cousin, Richie, who's a priest out in Queens. The guy drives a better car than mine. Always getting these expensive gifts. I asked him about it. Said he's got to beat the women off with a stick."

"Sounds like a true man of God."

"Yeah. Besides, I'm through with sex. It ain't all that it's cracked up to be. Too much investment for a few minutes of return."

"I see your point."

"Dave tells me that Ollie was the guy sending the notes and making the phone calls. How fucked-up is that?"

"I guess the roaches feasted on huge hunks of his brain."

"But he made confession, and everything's hunky-dory now."

"I'm sure it cost him a couple of Hail Marys and a few Our Fathers."

"If it was me sitting in the box listening to his bullshit, I'd've pulled him through the grill and beaten him to death."

"Your mother was right," I said. "You were definitely called to the priesthood."

"You don't give a crazy fucker like that absolution, you whack him in the head with a shovel and bury him in the woods."

"According to the map, we're coming up to Hastings-on-Hudson," I said. "Dobbs Ferry should be the next town."

"What do you make of Barak?" Nick said.

"What would you do if one of your kids were snatched?"

"Depends which one."

"Seriously."

"I am being serious. Nah. Barak made a deal. If he breaks it, he's in a world of shit."

"What is it, honor among thieves?"

"Something like that. What do you think Dave is going to do?"

"Kill the Golem," I said. "Before he kills Dave."

"Won't be easy. He's one tough son of a bitch. And smart. Not the kind of moron we ordinarily get to deal with."

"Dave shouldn't have taken his son," I said.

"I told him the same thing, but your brother keeps his own counsel. You know how he is."

I certainly did.

"There's the exit. Take a left at the light. That puts us on

Ashford Avenue. We take it a few miles until it becomes Broadway. She lives at 4300 Broadway. It's a straight shot."

We drove along Broadway until we hit Hastings.

"There's no 4300," I said.

"You probably missed it. I'll turn around, and we'll try it again. Pay attention this time."

Nick drove slower this time, with the same result. We pulled into a filling station. There was no 4300 Broadway.

"Now I'm pissed off," Nick said. "Clarkson better get their insurance policies ready."

"It's not their fault. She gave them a phony address."

"Where the hell could she be?" Nick said.

"In the wind. Or in a grave."

"Get your map out, and see how far away Tarrytown Road in White Plains is."

"Why?"

"So the day's not a total loss, I hear there's a great Italian restaurant over there. La Manda. Let's do it."

We did. And it was.

It was late afternoon when we got back to the city, and my best hope for the right string had evaporated. And it was no one's fault but my own. I hadn't done the basics with finding Lisa, and now it might be too late. Maybe Toal was right. I had been out of the game too long.

I called Lou Torricelli.

"Lou," I said, "Lisa is still missing, and I'm starting to worry. Have you heard from her?"

"Not a word. Like I told you, she took a leave."

"Does she have any family? Did she leave an emergency contact in her file?"

"Not that I know of, but give me a minute, and I'll pull it up on the screen. There it is. No. No family or next of kin. No emergency contact. Sorry."

"Does she have any friends at the office? Someone she goes to lunch with?"

"Lisa? She keeps to herself. To tell you the truth, the other women really don't like her much."

"Why is that?"

"She's young, pretty. You know. They kind of resent her."

Terrific! So much for the basics.

I decided to go home and take a nap.

Two hours later, I was up and not the least bit refreshed. I showered and shaved, but it didn't help. I was definitely in need of a change of pace.

My telephone rang. I picked it up.

"Steeg, it's Danny."

He wasn't the change of pace I had in mind.

"Did you get the money?"

"That's what I wanted to talk to you about. I wired it back to you."

"Why?"

"I don't need it."

"But you said . . ."

"I know what I said, and I appreciate everything you did for me. But I can't go along with the deal you and Dave cut."

"What are you telling me?"

"I wasn't totally honest with you. I got some money put aside. Doesn't exactly cover the principal and vig I owe Barak, but it'll have to do. Hey, he never thought he'd see any of it, right?"

I heard the tiny little feet of the possum trotting over my grave again.

"Danny . . ."

"Let me finish. I can't stay away from the city. It's like a jones. I gotta come home."

"He'll kill you. Trust me."

"He's a businessman first. With guys like him, it's all about money. I called him. Made him an offer. Got the certified check in my pocket. He's cool with it."

"They dragged Liam behind a car."

"Liam was an asshole and a hype. I'll be fine. Thanks again for being there for me. I'll never forget it."

There was a click, and the phone went dead.

There was nothing more to say, anyway.

I left my apartment, walked down the two flights of stairs, and knocked on DeeDee's door.

She was wearing shorts and a T-shirt, and her hair was pulled back in a ponytail.

"Do you want to have dinner?"

"If it's Feeney's, no. How's Allie?"

"We're back together."

"Should I be happy?"

"Yes."

"Good. I really like her. Where do you want to go?"

"Why didn't you say so?"

"You never asked," she said. "Now, where were we?"

"Dinner. How about Japanese?"

When we first started palling around, dinner—or any meal, for that matter—was a hit-or-miss proposition for DeeDee. With her mother in the wind, her father in the slam, and truancy elevated to high art, DeeDee was about to crater. That's when I hit on the idea of a foods-of-the-world tour of Hell's Kitchen restaurants. Several nights a week we'd try a new cuisine, and while we ate, I managed to slip a little history, geography, and culture into the conversation.

Two birds, one stone.

Now the lessons were over, but the tradition continued.

"Raw fish? Please!" she said, making a face. "They're crawling with bacteria. And haven't we evolved past chopsticks? If God wanted us to eat with wooden sticks, why would He have invented utensils?"

"They'll cook something for you and give you a fork."

"Fine," she said, sighing deeply.

We went to Kyoto, a hole-in-the-wall joint on Eleventh with six tables and the freshest fish in the city.

DeeDee ordered tempura, and I had the stuff crawling with bacteria.

When the food came, DeeDee glanced at my colorful plate with something approaching revulsion.

"I can't believe you ordered that," she said.

"Just living *la vida loca*."

She shook her head.

"What's bothering you, Steeg? Is it Allie?" she asked.

"I just spoke to a dead man."

"What do you mean?"

I gave her the highlights. Even I wasn't sure of the details anymore.

"There's nothing you can do about it, so why make yourself crazy?"

"It didn't have to happen this way. He was home free."

"No one is home free. My mother ran to the Dominican Republic to get away from my father. But she left me. She's not home free. What I'm saying is, there's always a cost. Depends how much you're willing to pay."

"How old are you?"

She smiled and her eyes lit up. "Fourteen going on thirty."

"How's your tempura?"

"Germ-free."

I flat-out loved this child.

After dinner I took DeeDee home, checked my messages—
there were none—and went to bed. I couldn't sleep and
was too tired to think. Too many hornets buzzing in my head.
Barak. Danny. Lisa. Dave. Ginny. Toal.

Toal!

I suddenly remembered my last conversation with Swede,
and it got me to thinking. Early the next morning I called him.

"This is Steeg."

"What do you want?"

"Remember where we met the last time?"

"Yeah."

"Could you be there in an hour?"

"Why?"

"I think we should talk."

"Talking to you is a waste of time," he said.

"Try me again."

This time Clinton Park wasn't empty. A couple of homeless
guys with cut-down cardboard boxes for mattresses stretched
out on benches, and the early-morning shift of dopers had
begun to line up for their first buy of the day.

We found an empty bench away from the madding crowd. I brought two containers of coffee and handed him one.

"I don't know how you like it, so it's black, no sugar," I said.

He took the container and pulled the tab on the lid.

"What's so important?"

"The last time we were here, you said I was fucking things up, that I should back away."

"So?"

"I assumed that you and Pete had a game going, and I was gumming up the works. But I was wrong, wasn't I?"

He took a sip of coffee and looked out at the river.

"Hot," he said.

"I asked you a question."

"From those to whom much is given, much is required. Would you agree?"

"Where's this going?"

His eyes scanned the junkies and homeless men.

"Take them, for example. The least of us. The throwaways. Who looks out for them?"

"What's your point?"

"We do, Steeg, because we took an oath. We look out for them just like we look out for everyone. No favorites. Everyone gets treated equally."

"That's the way it's supposed to work."

"But not always. And then you know what you got?"

"A bad cop," I said.

He finished his coffee and threw the cup in a garbage can.

"Worse," he said. "You got a rogue cop."

"You're IAD. The Rat Squad."

"Pejoratives will get you nowhere. The only reason I'm

telling you this is because I checked you out. I'm told I can trust you. For some reason that escapes me, there actually are people in the department who think you're worth a shit."

"I earned it the hard way."

"Maybe. With me, the jury is still out."

"With me too. But when you get right down to it, you haven't exactly covered yourself with glory."

"You don't give an inch, do you, Steeg?"

"Why should I?"

"We're building a case that could have far-reaching implications, and that's all I can say."

"So you're not talking the occasional—"

"What part of 'that's all I can say' didn't you understand? The best thing you can do is stay the hell away from him. You don't want to get caught in the crossfire. Do I make myself clear?"

"Actually, no. 'Far-reaching implications' is the crap you use to brush off some local news jock. Don't try it on me. I've earned my stripes."

He shrugged as if to say that from here on it was my funeral.

"Have it your way, Steeg. But don't come bitching to me if bad things begin to happen."

Bad things had already happened. A few more came with the territory.

The real business of Hell's Kitchen is hatched in its cracks and shadows. But the shadows were beginning to lift.

Swede and his bosses were building a case. Although he didn't say against whom, he didn't have to. Toal had filled in that blank. Two seemingly innocuous remarks, weeks apart, yet, when taken together, the sunlight poked through. That was the maddening fact of the Universe. Rarely did anything emerge fully formed. It revealed things in bits and pieces. And you had to pay attention.

I called Kenny and asked him to meet me at Feeney's. Turned out he was already there.

"Any progress on who owns Été?"

"As a matter of fact, there is," he said. "Not that it's very useful. It's a close corporation, and there's just one name and address listed."

"And he is?"

"A very big-time lawyer who wouldn't talk even if you held a gun to his children's heads."

"So where does that leave us?"

"Basically, nowhere."

"I thought you're an accountant."

"An accountant, yes. A magician, no. What can I tell you?"

"What would you say if I told you that I've succeeded where you've failed, Kenny my boy?"

"Really."

"I think I can identify at least one owner of that star-crossed restaurant."

Dave walked in and joined us. He had three men with him. One took up a position near the door, the other two sat at the bar.

"But," I said, "it's something we'll have to take up later."

"Jake. Kenny," Dave said.

"I heard from Danny Reno last night," I said.

"He call to thank you for saving his ass?"

"Not quite. Apparently you were right."

"About what?"

"He had some money put away."

"What a shock."

"He's giving it to Barak. Figures Barak will ease up and let him come back."

"Sweet Jesus! Barak doesn't want Reno's money, he wants his balls on a plate."

"Danny thinks otherwise. He said he was delivering the certified check last night."

"Does everyone you know have this need to wind up dead? It's like a reverse Midas touch."

"Why do you think that is?" I said.

"Like I said, you're a changeling. Only thing that explains it. The fairies dropped you off and took my real brother."

"Have Franny and the kids come back yet?"

"Things are still a little unsettled. Barak got to Liam's two pals."

"The guys who were hijacking merchandise for Reno?"

He nodded.

"The fucker sure knows how to carry a grudge. Seems he's working his way up the food chain."

"Which explains the three guys you brought with you," I said.

"You know where I kept his kid? In my house. In Anthony's room. It's like a pleasure dome. Has everything a boy could want. Took care of him like he was my own."

Dave's failure to appreciate the enormity of what he had done was beginning to get on my nerves.

"Don't you get it, Dave? You snatched his son! What if the shoe were on the other foot?"

"It would be a come-to-Jesus moment. Literally."

"And there you have it."

He grinned.

"Your problem is, you worry too much," Dave said.

"And your problem is, you're a thick-headed Mick."

"The Steeg family curse," Dave said. "I went looking for Barak. Kind of a preemptive strike. But he vanished. Has one of those houses as big as a cruise ship in Manhattan Beach. It's empty now. The club in Brighton Beach? They never heard of him. It's like trying to wrestle with mist. It's gonna be fun."

"Fun? Is this a game for you?"

"You really have to lighten up, Jake."

"Remember what Kenny said about the original golem?"

"No."

"He was just a pile of mud sleeping on a riverbank, until he was roused. When you kidnapped Barak's son, you woke him."

"So?"

"You loosed the killing machine."

It was a long time coming, but I finally figured out what made my brother tick.

To contextualize and explain who we are, we all—peoples and individuals—concoct our own creation myths. First we try them on to see if they fit, and then we tinker with them until they do. Dave's myth was that he was Dominic's son—another way of saying that brutishness begets brutishness, and that total disregard for accepted behavioral norms is a matter of unequal parts of nature and nurture. The truth is that my brother always had a skewed view of his place in the world, and Dominic, while not anyone's idea of a model dad, was close to, but not quite, the monster of Dave's imaginings.

Dave's sheer excitement at going head-to-head with Barak was the tip-off. Fun, Dave called it. And all at once, everything became clear. Dave was an adrenaline junkie between fixes. He needed the rush of neurons firing on overdrive that only a skydive with Barak could provide.

It had been a long time since Dave had really been tested. Organized crime is an oxymoron, populated with imbeciles devoid of artfulness and intelligence.

The kidnapping had put Dave and Barak into free fall. The real test was who would pull the rip cord first.

It was a question I couldn't answer.

Dave left and took Kenny with him. One more gun to tilt the odds. My brother may have been rocketing toward the ground, but he wasn't stupid.

I figured I'd pay Terry Sloan a visit.

■

The Hudson Democratic Club was crowded. Ten card tables were set up around the room, each manned by a guy with a clipboard. Standing around each table were knots of people listening intently to the guys with the clipboards.

Albert Mallus, Terry Sloan's dark eminence, stood in the center, looking on.

"Hello, Albert."

"Oh, Jesus! What the hell do you want?"

"What's going on, having a tag sale on some city assets?"

"Very funny. This is an election year. Gotta get a jump on things. As we speak, precinct captains are organizing the troops."

"Democracy in action. Does my heart good. Terry around?"

"No."

"Where is he?"

"Somewhere."

"Don't push it, Albert. I'm on a short fuse these days. He goes where you send him."

He made a face.

"Short fuse! What else is new?" Mallus said. "Terry is meeting with some developers. They're thinking about building offices and apartments over the Hudson Yards."

"Didn't that die when the Jets tried to build a stadium there?"

"That was just a first shot across the bow. Thanks to the foresight of our city leaders, the dream continues. We're talking decking over the rail yards and putting up parks, and other shit like that." His lips curled into a shit-eating grin. "You gotta think of the kids, Steeg. They're our future."

"Of course, the kids. A noble sentiment. And that means private money," I said.

"Just greasing the wheels of progress."

"And Terry is in the thick of things."

"He's a man who cares about the future of his constituents. The project means jobs for the neighborhood, so the working-man can hold his head up high. The American Dream."

"And an inground pool and sauna for Terry's new digs in the Hamptons."

"You're a cynic, Steeg."

"Sometimes the load gets too heavy to bear. I had lunch at Purslane the other day. Interesting place. Terry said he was going to open a few more."

"Why not? People got to eat. Even if the food tastes like crap. It's amazing, isn't it? The smaller the portions, the more you can charge. And the hotter the place. Go figure."

"How's his investment in Été working out?"

A few rapid blinks told me I had hit the mark.

"What are you talking about?" he said.

"What's there to hide, Albert? No one expects the man to live on his city council paycheck alone."

"I don't know anything about that. Look, it's been swell chatting, but I gotta get back to work."

"Just one more thing. Why did you have Banas, the waiter at Été, fired? What did he do to piss Terry off?"

"I don't know what you're looking for, Steeg, but you're not going to find it here."

"I'm almost there, my friend. And when I do find it, there's going to be hell to pay."

I almost believed it myself.

A s I left Mallus, I felt an urgent need for a shower. Hacks like Sloan and their acolytes believe that elected office is simply a socially convenient form of kingship, endowing them with the divine right to feed at the public trough like an all-you-can-eat buffet. But were they any different from my brother and Barak? Those two predators viewed the world as if it were their own private savannah and the rest of us were dinner.

My mood was not improved when I arrived home to find Barak waiting outside. Alone.

"Hello, Mr. Steeg."

"Where's Danny?"

"Your Mr. Reno is with us," he said.

"What does that mean?"

"Exactly what I said."

"He paid you the money, didn't he?"

"He did. Two hundred and fifty thousand. Unfortunately, he is a bit short."

"How short?"

"Seven hundred and fifty thousand dollars."

"So, consider it a good-faith down payment. He could have skipped. And then you would have nothing. But he didn't. Think of it as a third of a loaf. Forget about the vig, and you've got your original investment back."

"Then I would have made no profit. I would be a very poor businessman to accept those terms. Are you willing to be surety for the balance?"

"It's a little steep, Barak."

His lips stretched over his teeth in a poor imitation of a smile. "Very smart. One who stands surety for another is a fool. And you are not a fool, Mr. Steeg."

"When are you going to let him come home?"

"All in good time, Mr. Steeg."

I was tired of sparring with the man. "When is this going to end, Barak?"

"Why don't you ask your brother?"

"It's a waste of time. That's why I'm asking you."

"Our holy books say, 'In the mouth of the foolish is a rod of pride, but the lips of the wise shall preserve them.'"

"What the hell does that mean?"

He laughed. "You are an honest man, Mr. Steeg. What is on your mind is on your lips. A rarity in my business."

"Here's another dose of honesty. You and my brother make me sick. You're both killers pretending to be human beings. All you're really interested in is who has the biggest dick. And what really gets to me is that you don't give a shit that when the elephants dance, whoever's in the way gets his ticket punched."

Barak put his hands together and soundlessly clapped. "Bravo, Mr. Steeg! You have found us out. And now, what do you do with this great insight?"

"I love my brother, as much as your child loves you. He's all the family I have, and I don't want to lose him. I'll talk to him, convince him to walk away."

"I'm afraid your words will fall on deaf ears."

"How about you, Barak?"

"Remember what I said, Mr. Steeg, and take heed. The elephants are preparing to dance."

CHAPTER 48

I went up to my apartment to lie down. My chest was burning from the bullshit. Barak quotes scripture, but God's mercy isn't part of his makeup. Dave wears the guise of a family man and thinks nothing of kidnapping a child. Terry is supposed to be a public servant, but he forgot about the *servant* part. Then there was Ginny, my biggest disappointment. And all of it was somehow linked.

I was close; so close that I had become a target. For all of Barak's profession of love and respect, the guy was a psychopath. He had his son back—and he had Danny Reno—but he wasn't quite done yet. Wasn't quite ready to ride off into the sunset. In his fucked-up mind, Dave and I were linked. If Dave went, I was a loose end who would have to go too. And then there was my old drinking buddy, Toal. Whose sun was I flying too close to?

The prospect of no good outcomes ignited an urgent dryness in the back of my throat, putting the nasty critters that live in my head in a black mood. The snakes were hot to trot, and I was along for the ride.

I count myself among those drunks who, even though

sober for years, keep a bottle of their favorite stuff handy. It's kind of a final exam for those moments when you're out of good reasons to keep hanging on to the planet by your finger-nails. A moment when you simply say "Fuck it!" It's a test I've failed three or four times in the few years I've been clear-eyed.

I went into my bedroom, opened the drawer of my night table, pulled out a bottle of Aberlour, and the Glock lying be-side it. The Glock, like the Aberlour, was a daily test of my re-solve, as well as a Steeg family tradition. Aberlour single malt Scotch whiskey was my father's beverage of choice and his last drink before he jammed his service revolver in his mouth and pasted his brains against the wall. A final toast to a squan-dered life.

I lifted the bottle and turned it in my hand, teasing the cap with my fingers, hypnotized by how the dusky light turned the dark amber liquid to soft gold. My mouth had turned to sand. I eased the cap off, closed my eyes, and the aroma of peat mixed with honey and oaken sherry and damp grass made me dizzy.

I stumbled to the bed and sat staring at the bottle, imagin-ing the punch of molten sweetness slamming into the back of my throat and the numbing darkness it brought in its wake. My hands trembled with anticipation.

My gaze fell on the Glock. I picked it up. The Aberlour in my left hand, and the Glock in my right.

Options.

The lady, or the tiger? A sucker's choice.

A loser's choice.

I closed the cap tight, put the Glock back in the night table, and stretched out on the bed. Still nestling the bottle against my chest, I dropped into a fitful sleep and dreamed jumbled, quick-cut, dry-drunk dreams roiling with sinners, their black eyes burning with a mad fire, elbowing their way onto center stage, eager for their star turn.

Later—minutes, hours? I had no idea—I awoke to the sound of tumblers snapping. Suddenly, my apartment door opened. A small shaft of light knifed into the living room. And just as quickly disappeared. Then, the sound of footsteps—soft, puffy, magnified by the silence—on the wooden floor.

Rubbing the sleep from my eyes, I eased the Glock from its drawer and waited. Heart beating like a Gene Krupa drum riff.

The footsteps stopped. The outline of a man filled the bedroom doorway. Something in his hand glinted in the dim light filtering up from the street.

I aimed the Glock at his midsection.

He took a shooter's stance.

My finger closed on the trigger, releasing and closing until the clip emptied.

Like a scrap of paper caught on a rising wind, he blew backward into my living room.

I flipped on the light and walked over to him. He was on his back. His chest shredded. His left leg splayed in an impossible position. The throwaway gun still clenched in his fist.

I knelt down and pressed my index finger to his carotid artery.

No pulse.

I didn't expect any.

The final piece had fallen into place.

I called Swede.

"I just killed Pete Toal," I said. "My apartment."

The silence lasted a few seconds.

"I'll be right over," he finally said. "Don't do anything. I'll call it in."

Twenty minutes later, Swede arrived with a surprisingly small crew in tow—the ME, two crime-scene investigators, and one uniformed sergeant to tape and seal the apartment. It struck me as odd. A killing tends to attract lots of brass looking for face time with the press. But there wasn't a media type around.

The crew set about doing their jobs with very little chatter and lots of urgency.

"How come you didn't bring the cavalry?" I said. "Short-staffed?"

"We're kind of keeping a lid on this," Swede said, tight-lipped. "Where's your piece?"

I handed it to him. He dropped it in a plastic bag, sealed it, and handed it to one of the uniforms, mumbling something about preserving the chain of evidence.

Then he looked down at Toal, shook his head in disgust, and turned back to me.

"Fuck him! Let's get a cup of coffee while they clean up the mess."

We headed for a diner on Tenth Avenue. At two in the morning, business was brisk despite the rain. We found a booth in the back and ordered.

"What the hell happened?"

I told him.

"We were looking at Toal. Suspected him of all sorts of fuckaround but were on 'wait and watch' mode. Figured he'd lead us to more important people of interest."

"People of interest?"

"His masters. But you screwed the pooch when you killed him, Steeg. The official line will be, the investigation continues, but without him we've got jack. And the scumbag gets an inspector's funeral. That's one of the things I hate about this job. Everything's upside down."

A few strings were finally coming together. "Maybe the pooch is still a virgin."

The coffee came. Swede waited until the waitress left before he spoke. "I'm listening," he said.

"How closely are you looking at Terry Sloan?"

His eyes narrowed. "What made you pluck his name out of the hat?" he asked.

"The only name that makes sense."

He planted his arms on the table and leaned forward.

"OK," he said. "What have you got?"

"You first."

He gave a resigned shake of his head. "Why not?" he said. "That fucking sleazeball Sloan is the primary focus of our investigation. We believe the councilman is wetting his beak on city construction contracts, and Toal was his bagman. We were close to nailing him, and then you take Toal—our best shot at someone on the inside—out of the world."

"Did you talk to the contractors?"

"Now, that's a major whoop," he said. "Even with promises of immunity, they become mute when we walk in the door."

"So you don't even have enough for probable cause."

"Fuck probable cause. We'd have to have a bulletproof case. Who picks the fucking judges?"

"The bosses, like Sloan."

"Right! And it's a small, tight-knit fraternity. These guys aren't going to bite the hand that puts them on the ballot un-opposed year after year, not unless we leave them with no choice."

"Would a murder charge help?"

"You've got my attention," he said.

"Why did Pete come gunning for me?"

"Are you saying Sloan ordered Toal to hit you?"

"No, Terry would never do that. He knows Dave would strangle him with his own intestines. Toal acted on his own, bucking Sloan's orders to lay off me. Toal's world was coming apart. He knew it was just a matter of time before I nailed him for Noonan's murder, and maybe even Ferris's. And that would lead back to Terry. He simply had too much to lose by letting me live."

"And the collateral benefit to Sloan was that with you out of the way, it would be back to business as usual." He paused to consider this. "Could be."

"And Toal would be an even fairer-haired boy in Terry's eyes," I said. "And that translates to more money in the bank."

Swede nodded.

"And that's your theory," he said, taking a sip of coffee. "Interesting."

"And I'm sticking to it."

Swede leaned back and a smile crossed his lips.

"One thing's for sure, Steeg. You certainly lead a convoluted life."

Things were pretty quiet over the next two days. On the third day, everything changed. Dave called. He wanted to talk.

We met in Clinton Park. A full-court basketball game was in progress nearby. The day was warm, and they were sweating. One guy, a tall Hispanic, was a cut above the other players. He knew it and hogged the ball.

We watched for a few minutes.

"He's good," I said.

"Yeah, but not a team player. That's why he and his buddies are gonna lose."

"Maybe," I said. "The other guys aren't exactly all-stars."

"Yeah, but they're playing together, and in the end, teamwork is the key."

We found a bench and sat down. Dave's guys formed a loose perimeter around us. Kenny wasn't among them.

It occurred to me that Barak went about his business alone. Round one to Barak.

"What's on your mind, Dave?"

"You."

"You want to expand on that a little?"

"You've got a big mouth, Jake."

"That's not new news, Dave."

"But this time you went too far. You've been talking to the cops about Terry."

Why bother to deny it?

"You've got somebody in IAD," I said.

"You're surprised? Come on, Jake! I've got somebody everywhere. Terry's very unhappy."

"Good. Every time I can make that prick frown, another angel is born."

"What the fuck is wrong with you?"

"Let's call it an aversion to slime."

"What's that supposed to mean?"

"I'm tired of slime. Tired of rubbing shoulders with it, tired of reading about it, tired of being around it. Maybe we put all of them—crooked CEOs, judges and politicians with their hands out, child molesters and rapists—in a cage and let them fight to the death in a Last Man Standing event."

"Put it on pay-per-view. It would be a moneymaker."

"Look, I'm no Mother Teresa, but some things just make you gag, and I can't fix them. But there are a few things I can fix. And Terry Sloan is one of them. He had Noonan killed. I don't know the reason yet, but I will."

"Even if you fuck something up for me?" Dave said.

Now, that was something I hadn't thought of.

"Don't tell me you're involved in this."

"Interesting word, *involved*. Lot of leeway in there. Let's just say that I have a financial interest in Terry's enterprises. And you poking around might put them, and me, at risk."

"It's only money," I said.

"Lots of it, actually.

"Why was Noonan killed?"

"I don't know."

"How about Ferris?"

"Same answer."

"Don't you think it's just a wee bit strange that Été was the common thread of two murders?"

"Hell of a coincidence, I'll give you that."

"Why is it coincidences spontaneously occur when reason is absent?"

"Jake, you're in over your head here, and I don't know that I'll be able to protect you."

"From Sloan? You have to be kidding."

"No, he's the front man. The shoeshine and a smile. I'm talking heavy hitters, the guys who play Monopoly with real money. They've got a lot at stake and aren't about to let you piss in the punch."

"Then I'll have to deal with it."

"It's not as simple as that. For all I know, they have guys like Barak on retainer."

"Dave, I'm past the point of caring."

"Terry is going to walk, Jake. You know that, don't you? It'll never even get to an arraignment, much less a trial."

"You're probably right, but at least he'll have a few days of throwing up."

"Is it worth it?"

"We all choose the hills we want to die on."

"That we do."

"I've got one more question."

"Sure."

"Why was Noonan killed?"

"You never let go, do you?"

"Would you?"

"He saw something he shouldn't have."

"And Toal was cleaning up the mess?"

"No more questions."

After Dave left, I wandered over to the basketball court and watched the game. Dave was right. It was all about teamwork. The Hispanic guy was good, and that was his Achilles' heel. His team was heading into the tank.

Strings.

They were everywhere. Crossing. Looping. Tangling. And with each day, new strings emerged. New tangles. New dead ends. It made my head hurt.

I left the park and walked to the river. There was a stiff breeze, and out on the water the few sailboats skipped over the light chop. Overhead, gulls hovered on the updrafts, keeping a keen eye out for a snack. And I was searching for a string. It was like playing cat's cradle with one hand. Suddenly I realized that was the problem. I called Luce and asked her to meet me.

"Where will you be?" she said.

"Do you know the Trapeze School down on West Street?"

"Sure. Why there?"

"I'm tired of flying without a net and falling flat on my face. Figured I'd learn how it's done."

"Can I ask why the urgency?" she said.

"I need you to play cat's cradle with me."

A half hour later she arrived.

"The only reason I'm here is that I'm beginning to wonder about your sanity, Jackson," she said.

"And here I was thinking it was love."

"There's that, and if I ever get a hankering for men, you'd be at the top of my list. But even you have to admit that you sounded totally nuts. Figured that erasing Toal maybe got you a bit off-kilter. By the way, no one's talking about the shooting. Care to share?"

"All in good time."

She sighed. "It's hard having a friend who refuses to gossip, Jackson. It just ain't normal."

I shrugged. "What can I tell you?"

"Fine. You wanted to play cat's cradle, and I'm here. So . . ."

"Actually, what I had in mind was a virtual version of the game." I explained my dilemma.

"So you need help thinking through the maze."

"Something like that."

"Why didn't you say so?"

"Then I'd have to admit that I needed help. Well, maybe not help exactly. Let's call it confirmation."

She threw her hands up in disgust. "You really try me, Jackson. Where do you want to start?"

"At the beginning, with the looped string."

"And that is?"

"Tons of real-estate development money. Here's how it works. The city lets a truly obscene amount of money in construction contracts every year."

"Makes sense. New York is growing in population. The old buildings need remodeling, and you need new buildings to accommodate the growth. This isn't new news, Jackson."

"But certain elected officials use these construction funds as their own personal piggy bank by gaming the rules."

"Also not new news, but getting a whole lot more interesting," Luce said.

"The funds are not allocated arbitrarily. To protect the rights of minority-owned businesses and to ensure that they get a slice of the pie, there's something called the Minority Opportunities Bureau. It's the approving agency for all contracts."

"Power to the people!"

"Not quite. I have reason to believe the bureau is the piggy bank for Councilman Terry Sloan and his friends."

"So, some whitey fat cats are fucking my people over again. What a surprise! Martin Luther King must be spinning in his grave."

"Here's the kicker. Ferris was the number-two guy in the bureau."

She feigned shock. "A brother screwing over other brothers? Where will it end?"

"It's good to see that you're emotionally invested in this. May I continue?"

"Please."

"Ferris had a boss, one Lou Torricelli."

"The token white guy. Is he screwing over the brothers too?"

"I don't know. But let me throw a few more strings into the mix. Ginny and Ollie."

"The ex-wife and Mr. Skinhead."

"The very same. Let's start with Ginny. Turns out she and Ferris are in an open marriage."

"Come on! That sweet little thing?"

"People change."

"I'm just opining here, but could it be her new boyfriend took the whole thing too seriously and figured he'd remove an obstacle to true and enduring love?"

"Actually, they were each other's alibi. Ginny claimed that they were together the night Ferris was killed."

"The vixen."

"I spoke to the guy. Works in the city. An attorney. Doesn't seem the type to kill anyone. Seemed more frightened of his wife finding out than going down on a murder charge."

"And that leaves us with Ollie," Luce said. "Didn't he send those notes and make those phone calls?"

"He did. But what's really strange is that Torricelli got some threatening phone calls also. Why would Ollie do that?"

"Maybe to get Ferris fired?" Luce said.

I made a mental note to ask Ollie about that.

"Ready for another string?" I said.

"I'm running out of fingers here, but go ahead."

"Lisa Hernandez, Ferris's assistant."

"Where does she come in?"

"Shortly after Ferris is killed, she packs up and hightails it to parts unknown. Takes a leave of absence from her job."

"Maybe the poor thing was so shaken by the violence that befell her boss that she's off grieving somewhere."

"She didn't leave a forwarding address," I said.

"Let me restate my last thought. She's either scared shitless, or the bitch is up to her ears in Ferris's murder."

"Exactly my thought. I make her for Ferris's dinner companion. She was there the night he was killed as either a witness or a party to the act."

"A reasonable leap of logic, Jackson. Please tell me you're out of strings."

"Just a few more."

"Can we eat while we play?"

"Sure."

I picked up a couple of hot dogs and Diet Cokes from a nearby stand.

"First that roach palace up in the Bronx," she said, "and now this. You surely know the way to a girl's heart. And you even remembered to bring napkins. My, my."

"Wouldn't want you to get mustard all over your pretty new suit. Now, where were we?"

"More strings."

"Right. That brings us to Noonan."

"The guy who worked at Été until he was murdered."

"The very same," I said. "Turns out that Terry Sloan owns a piece of the restaurant."

"It's good to put your crooked money to work, especially in a restaurant where Ferris had his last meal."

"According to Dave . . ."

"Oh my! Is he involved in this too?"

"Let's keep moving. Noonan was iced because he saw something he shouldn't have."

"Could it be Ferris and his dinner partner? Or did he witness the murder?"

"Ferris was killed out in the alley. Noonan worked inside. It was a busy night."

"Maybe he went out for a smoke," Luce said. "It's easy enough to check."

I pulled my cell phone out, called Stuart, and put him on speaker. I asked him if Noonan was a smoker. He wasn't.

"I love a man who takes control of a situation, Jackson. Just like that, you called the man and cleared things up. So, Noonan saw Ferris and his dinner companion, and could identify said person. And that could lead to everything unraveling."

We were on the same track.

"Keep going," I said.

"Because you were the real problem, Jackson. Sloan knew you were involved in the investigation and would walk the cat back to him. The easy fix was to get rid of you, but if he did, Dave would cut him up into little pieces. It was no accident that Toal was the lead detective on Ferris's murder."

Toal was right—in a way, I was on Dave's pad. Not a pleasant thought.

"Exactly. Terry was his rabbi," I said. "He's the guy who put Toal in Anti-Terrorism, and then popped him into Homicide when I retired. Toal was Terry's lapdog."

"Bingo!"

"It gets better," I said. "Toal mentioned that he had a high-paying security job lined up when he retired. I'll bet Terry arranged it. And Toal returned the favor by doing Noonan.

"What started as a simple scheme to steal money defied the laws of moral gravity and spun out of control," I continued. "I told you we'd get around to Toal in good time."

"And you're a man of your word. I wonder who the mystery man who got Banas fired was?" Luce said.

"It had to be Terry's guy, Albert Mallus. He's made a career of cleaning up after the councilman."

Except for a few details easy enough to check, it all made sense. All I needed was some hard evidence to fit the theory.

"We make a pretty good pair," I said.

Luce leaned over and kissed my forehead. "Like Sherlock and Watson," she said.

And the game was afoot.

I was on my way to Feeney's when my cell phone rang. It turned out to be my old friend Rosie Alba, Lisa Hernandez's nosy neighbor.

"I called to thank you," she said.

"For what?"

"I got that paint job. Wasn't for you, it never would have happened."

"Glad to help, Ms. Alba."

"Call me Rosie. You're almost a member of the family now."

I could hear the smile in her voice.

"Appreciate it."

"By the way. I saw the Hernandez slut. I was over at the post office, and she was there, pissin' and moanin' about something or other."

"Was she alone?"

She chuckled. "Yeah, right. That one is never alone, if you know what I mean. With an older guy. Seemed kind of embarrassed by the scene she was making."

"When was this, Rosie?"

"This morning, about twenty minutes ago. He acted like he was in a hurry. Kept saying he had to get back to work. She didn't seem to care much, like she had all the time in the world."

"Have you seen him with Lisa before?"

"A lot," she said.

"Can you describe him?"

"Overweight. Balding. Looks like one of those guys you see working at the Welfare office."

"Rosie, you are the best."

"It's gonna be peach."

She lost me. "What is?"

"The paint job. Everything is gonna be peach."

I hung up and called Swede.

"I'm about to make your career," I said.

■

I met Swede at Midtown North. It was the first time I had ever seen him smile.

"I have to admit, this is turning into one of those moments that I just live for," he said.

"But you needed lots of convincing."

"That I did, but with the Sloan investigation conducted by very careful people above my pay grade, I didn't have a whole lot else going on, so why not take a flyer. They were just leaving his office when I got there."

"Timing is everything. Are they talking?"

"Not long in coming. This is their first swing through the system, and they're dazed at being yanked out of their world into mine. I would invite you to the party, but . . ."

"I'm not a cop anymore. I understand."

"But," Swede said, "I've got a front-row seat with your name on it behind the two-way mirror."

"I appreciate it. You've got them together?"

"Oh yeah. And Mirandized. I can't wait to see who throws the other under the bus first."

"I'm betting it's Lisa. I don't see her as the stand-by-your-man type."

"Looking down the barrel of a long stretch at Bedford Hills does tend to force one to rethink things. It could be a long afternoon. You want a cup of coffee or something?"

"I'm good."

"Then it's showtime."

▪

The interview room was spartan and brightly lit. Table. Four folding chairs. Wastepaper basket.

Lisa Hernandez and Lou Torricelli sat with their chairs angled away from each other.

"Is everyone comfortable? Need some coffee?" Swede asked.

Neither responded.

"Why are we here?" Torricelli finally said.

"Like I told you, Lou, I need a few questions answered, and then you're on your way. But they're serious questions, and it's important that you level with me."

"Level with you about what? You barge into my office and drag us—"

Torricelli still had some fight left . . . until Swede dropped the hammer.

"How about conspiracy, grand larceny, bribery of a public official, embezzlement of city funds, and the ever popular murder, for openers?"

I smiled as the expression on Torricelli's face moved from outrage to fear.

His voice was hesitant and small. "How did we go from a couple of questions and I'm on my way to . . . murder?"

Swede shrugged. "I lied, Lou."

It was Lou Torricelli's come-to-Jesus moment, the realization that his life had just hit a reef. He reached for the wastepaper basket and threw up.

Lisa made a face and turned away.

"I see I have your attention, Lou," Swede said. "It's a good thing."

Swede turned his attention to Lisa. "And after we finish with your boyfriend, you're up."

"I don't have nothing to do with nothing," she said. "I didn't do nothing wrong."

"Then you've got nothing to worry about," Swede said.

"I want a lawyer," Torricelli said, knowing that he was beyond help.

"That's your right, Lou. You can lawyer-up now and take your chances—which look mighty dim, if you ask me—or you can talk to me and help yourself out in the long run."

Torricelli pulled out a handkerchief and swiped it across his mouth. His face was pasty and damp with sweat, but his eyes lit up as if had he spotted a life raft bobbing nearby.

"What do you mean, 'help myself'?"

Swede walked over to him and laid his hand on his shoulder. "You have a family, Lou?"

"Yes."

."They're gonna miss you. You're looking at the needle for the Ferris murder," he said.

A little white lie, but entirely appropriate.

Torricelli made a grab for the wastepaper basket.

"I'm really sorry, Lou," Swede continued. "But if you're straight with me, we might be able to make that part go away. Might. No promises. Yet."

"How?"

"You give, and you get."

"What do you mean?"

"I know you murdered Ferris," Swede said, "but let's put that aside for now. Let's talk about who you conspired with to rob the taxpayers blind."

The light in Torricelli's eyes dimmed.

"You don't know who you're dealing with," he said. "They'll kill me if I talk."

Swede smiled. "And the state will kill you if you don't. Your choice."

The wastepaper basket was getting a hell of a workout.

Torricelli straightened up and hung his head in his hands.

"You'll protect . . . my . . . family?"

"You have my word."

"How good is that?"

"It's all you've got."

Torricelli took a very long time, and I didn't blame him.

He looked over at Lisa, but there was no help from that quarter, and I think he realized that there probably never was. Lou Torricelli was truly on his own.

"Here's how it worked," he finally said.

Swede patiently walked him through the scheme, and Torricelli spilled his guts, naming contractors, the size of the kickbacks—approximately $30 million—and to whom they flowed. Torricelli gave up some of the most powerful real-estate barons in the city.

And then Swede got to the good part. "Were there any city officials involved in the fraud?"

"Councilman Terry Sloan had a piece of every contract."

Have a happy Fourth, Terry!

"Did you deal with Councilman Sloan directly?"

"No. One of his associates. Albert Mallus. Everything went through him."

"Did you keep records of your transactions with Mallus and the others who were receiving payoffs?"

"I did. I keep them in a safe in my home."

Maybe there really was a God.

An hour later Swede was done with that phase of the interrogation. The DA had enough to keep his office busy for the next year. He moved on to Ferris.

"Why did you kill Ferris?"

Torricelli threw one last look at Lisa, but she refused to meet his gaze. He turned back to Swede. His voice was resigned.

"The son of a bitch was shorting me," he said. "Ferris dealt with the contractors. They paid him. He took his one percent and turned the rest over to me for disbursement. Everything worked fine for a while, until I noticed that something was wrong. The money didn't quite add up."

"So you confronted him?"

"Yeah, and he denied it. But I saw what was going on."

"And that was the reason you bashed his head in."

"Right."

"Lou, you're not being straight here," Swede said. "I saw you sneak a peek at Lisa. What was that all about?"

"Nothing. It's like I said. The guy was shorting me."

"How much money have you made to date? Roughly."

"Three million. Give or take."

"And how much was Ferris holding back? Roughly."

"Fifty, sixty thousand."

"Come on, Lou. With the money you banked, and the money that each new contract spun off, that's chump change. Certainly not enough to kill someone over."

Torricelli looked away.

"It was all about Lisa," Swede said, "wasn't it?"

"I don't know what you're talking about."

"You and Ferris were both on her A-list of, shall we say, companions. What happened, Lou, competition got a little stiff?"

His face reddened, but he remained silent.

"Then Ferris probably mentioned the threats he was getting, so you figured it would be a swell idea to tell Steeg that you were getting threats too. Right?"

Torricelli stared at the ceiling.

"How about it, Lisa?" Swede said. "Is that the way it went down? Is that what you and Tony were talking about at dinner the night Lou killed him?"

"No," she said. "I had no idea the sick bastard was gonna do what he did. The truth is, it didn't have to happen the way it did."

"Why not?"

"I told Lou that Tony and I were done. He would never leave his wife. But it didn't matter to Lou." She shot

Torricelli an icy look. "Every time he would see Tony, he'd get more and more jealous. I don't know why. Besides, Lou had all that money, and Tony didn't. So, for me, it was Lou all the way."

What's a girl to do?

Terry Sloan's perp walk made the front pages of all the morning newspapers. The sight of him in cuffs with his Armani jacket pulled over his head lifted my spirits to celestial heights. It was as close to heaven as I would ever get.

I was at my kitchen table, drinking coffee and savoring every word of the article detailing his comeuppance, when there was a knock at the door. It was Ginny and Jeanmarie.

With the barest of nods, Jeanmarie went to my cupboard, pulled out two cups, and poured herself and Ginny coffee. It was Jeanmarie being Jeanmarie, and I let it slide.

"You did good, Steeg," she said. "You caught the bastard and made things right. Not that you didn't have help, mind you."

Jeanmarie had lost nothing off her fastball. A compliment delivered without a commensurate dig was hardly worth the effort.

"Thank you, Jeanmarie."

"And you didn't want me to ask Steeg for help," she said to Ginny. "Who was right?"

"I'm grateful for what you did, Jake," Ginny said. "I know it was difficult for you."

"I'm just happy it worked out," I said.

"Where do you keep your sugar, Steeg?" Jeanmarie said. "This coffee is so strong the damn spoon stands up on its own."

"On the shelf above the cups."

Ginny smiled. "She is what she is," she said. "Never will change."

"It would make a lot of people happier if she did."

Jeanmarie found the sugar and returned to the table.

"That murderin' Italian swine, Torricelli," she said. "I want to be the last face the bastard sees when they give him the juice."

We all have a right to our fantasies.

"Mom," Ginny said. "Will you excuse us? I want to talk to Jake. Alone."

Jeanmarie shot Ginny a disapproving look.

"More secrets?" she said. "I believe that's what got you into trouble in the first place."

Ginny took my hand and led me toward the bedroom. She closed the door.

"Jeanmarie has a point," she said.

"That's not for me to say. Your life is your business."

"I'm sorry I got you into this mess."

"As I recall, it was Jeanmarie's idea."

"But if it weren't for me, none of this would have happened."

"If feeling guilty is a consolation, then go for it. I don't see it that way, Ginny. Tony was caught up in something that had nothing to do with your marriage. It took on its own momentum. Look, Lisa had already chosen Torricelli simply because she knew Tony wouldn't leave you. You can take some solace in that."

"What counts is that you were stand-up. Not a lot of ex-husbands would do that."

"Is there a future with you and potential husband number four?" I asked.

"He tells me you met him. What do you think?"

"Seems like a jerk."

She giggled. "He does, doesn't he?"

She took me in her arms and hugged tight.

"You know what I really regret?" she said.

"What?"

"Walking out on you. You were a keeper, Jake."

After that, there wasn't very much to say. She and Jean-marie finished their coffee and left. I headed over to Feeney's.

Feeney's had the joie de vivre of a tomb.

Dave sat in a back booth with three newspapers spread out on the table. Four of his men watched the door. He waved me over.

His finger stabbed at the headline. "Doesn't matter what I say, does it?" he said. "You just don't listen."

"Let's just say I'm tired of playing little brother. It's getting old."

He stared at me for a few seconds and then said, "What are you talking about?"

"Pete Toal said something a while ago that stuck with me. He said I was on your pad, and he was right."

"What pad? What the fuck are you talking about?"

"Where you barge into my life and I'm supposed to be grateful. Look, your business is something we never discussed."

"So?"

"We didn't discuss it because it never involved me. We built a firewall, and it worked. It's not working anymore. I never asked you to help with Danny Reno. That was your idea.

I'm looking for Ginny's husband's killer, and I'm afraid to look too hard. You know why? I might find you in there somewhere. It's a real problem, Dave."

"I was only looking out for you."

"I know that, but when you look out for me, people die. I know I put a crimp in your income. But you'll make it back. I put some of your friends in jail. You'll find new friends. But . . ."

"I'm not going to find a new brother," Dave said.

"Something like that."

"It's that serious?"

"Yeah."

He reached over and patted my face. "It took balls for you to say that, Jake."

"If I were one of your hired goons, it would have taken balls. But you keep forgetting that I don't work for you. I have genetic license to tell you you're full of shit and not have to worry that you're going to blow me away. Think of it as a life-long get-out-of-jail pass."

He smiled. "Franny has the other one." He held out his hand. "Point taken. You have my word. Are we square?"

I took his hand. "As long as you keep your end of the bargain," I said.

"Old habits are hard to break, but I'll work on it."

Nick brought over a pot of coffee and joined us.

"This thing is going to last two, maybe three days max, and then the reporters are on to the next thing," he said.

"I don't know about that," I said. "From what I saw, this is going to be the story that keeps on giving."

"You were there?" Dave said.

"As a voyeur. Swede extended some professional courtesy."

Dave pushed the newspapers aside. "So, we get to hear what went down straight from the horse's mouth. Good."

I took my time and gave them all the gory details. This was one story I didn't mind telling.

When I'd finished and sat back, Dave said, "By the way, the cops never found the set of books Torricelli claims he had stashed in his house."

I didn't even bother to ask where he got his information.

"Is that a fact?"

"Yep. You know who you remind me of, Jake?"

"Who?"

"That guy who spends eternity rolling a boulder uphill."

"Sisyphus."

"Yeah, that's the one. I told you, Jake, no one's gonna do any time. Oh, maybe a few lower-level guys get busted, but the bosses? No. And Terry? Without the books, he's the aggrieved party. You've turned him into the poster boy for malicious prosecution by political opponents bent on his destruction. All the cops have is Torricelli's word, and who's gonna believe a confessed murderer?"

I had a sudden sinking feeling.

"Pretty slick," I said.

"It gets even slicker. He's got the top PR firm in the city sprucing up his image. Wouldn't surprise me if he wins the Humanitarian of the Year Award."

"He's collecting on all his IOUs."

"Not all, but most. You watch a lot of television, Jake?"

"Some."

"Me, I like sitcoms. You know why?"

I shook my head.

"I figured them out," Dave said. "There's a formula, y'know."

"Really."

"No shit. Every week is the same as the week before. Everybody's happy, just like you left them, and then something happens and everything goes topsy-turvy. But by the end of every show, things settle back to normal. Nothing really changes."

"Your point?"

"By next week this will all be forgotten, and where will you be?"

"Sleeping better."

"Wise up, Jake. It's the way of the world."

"Have you talked to Terry?"

"Sure."

"Is he pissed?"

"You bet."

"Then I've done my job."

"You're a lost cause. The boulder is just gonna get heavier, and the slope steeper."

Suddenly, Dave's eyes went to the door. He stiffened. So did his gun dogs.

Barak was in the house. Alone. He carried what looked like a reddish orange, earthenware box. A couple of yards of duct tape secured the top to the container.

He walked up to us and set it on the table. Dave reached inside his jacket.

"I'm not armed," Barak said, lifting his arms. "Feel free to check."

Dave's hand came out of his jacket empty, but his men held their guns against their thighs.

"What the fuck are you doing here?" Dave said.

Barak smiled. "Bearding the lion in his den. I came to say good-bye. Your brother was very persuasive. There is nothing to be gained from our conflict."

Dave looked at me. "What's he talking about?" he said.

"I met him. We talked. Said you were both assholes who had severe penis problems. And then I forgot about it."

"Is that right, Barak?"

"Essentially."

"You're a regular Dale Carnegie, Jake."

"Your brother is an honest man."

"Funny. We've just been talking about that."

"I leave you this as a gift, a sign of my intentions. It is very old, and quite precious. Be very careful with it."

"Where's Danny Reno?" I said.

"I would like to discuss that with you, outside."

I followed him out to his car.

"Reno," I said.

"The gift I left with your brother is a museum piece. Dates from the time of Christ, perhaps earlier. It's called an ossuary."

The word sounded familiar, but I couldn't quite put my finger on it.

"Where's Danny?"

"He's already here."

I looked in the car. No Reno.

"Stop screwing with—"

I finally made the connection. An ossuary is a bone box.

And then I heard the roar.

I woke up on a gurney in Bellevue's emergency room. Turns out, I was far enough from the blast to avoid serious injury but close enough to screw up my lung even more. There was nothing the docs could do, but they kept me overnight for observation. I was one of the lucky ones. Two of Dave's men wound up in the morgue. Nick was OK—he'd been in the storeroom, out of harm's way. Dave was in intensive care.

The next morning, the docs discharged me. I went to see Dave. Franny and Anthony were at his bedside. Nick stood at the doorway.

"How is he?"

"You don't know?" Nick said.

"Only what the nurse said. His condition is critical."

"He lost his left hand. Blew it clean off."

"Sweet Jesus!"

"He nearly lost an eye, but they were able to save it. The way I heard it, Dave was bragging about Barak blinking first. Y'know, he figured he beat the bastard. Then he tried to open the box but there was so much duct tape, Dave went looking for a knife."

"Then he opens the lid," I muttered.

"Yeah. And the first thing he sees is—"

"Reno's head."

"Right. Dave slams the lid down and the bomb goes off. Must have used a time-delay fuse. And that's all she wrote. You OK?"

"In the pink. How badly was Feeney's damaged?"

"Pretty bad. But we're like Timex. Take a licking, but we keep on ticking. We'll be back."

"I've got to see my brother."

Franny and Anthony were at his bedside. Franny's eyes were swollen. Anthony, gritting his teeth, never took his eyes off his father. The stump where Dave's hand used to be was swathed in bandages.

"How is he?" I said.

"Not so good. He's all doped up. Sometimes he's awake, most often he's not. How are you?"

"I'm fine. What did the doc say?"

"He'll make it, but it's going to take time."

"I'm so sorry, Franny."

"I'm not surprised. His whole life was leading to this. You don't know how many times I begged him to quit. In a way, he's lucky it's just his hand."

"That fucking heeb is going to pay for this," Anthony muttered.

Suddenly, Franny wheeled and smacked him in the face. It was the first time I had ever seen her hit any of her children.

The skin around her eyes tightened. Her voice was cold and flat. "It ends here," she said.

For an instant, Anthony glared at her, then lowered his

eyes. I couldn't be sure, but I thought I saw the hint of a smile.

"Jake!"

Dave's voice was hoarse, and barely above a whisper. He motioned me over.

I put my hand on his forehead. It was clammy. His breathing was rapid.

"How're you doing, Dave?"

"Something to . . . tell . . . you."

I brought my ear to his mouth.

"Sins of . . . the . . . fathers . . ."

And then his eyes closed. He was breathing easier now that he had handed down his myth to his son.

"What did he say?" Franny asked.

"That he's sorry . . . sorry for everything."

ACKNOWLEDGMENTS

Stories may spring from a writer's head, but books are always the result of a collaboration. *Old Flame* is no exception. I would like to thank my agent, David Larabell of the David Black Agency, for never allowing me to veer off track when *off track* is exactly where I wanted to go; Julian Pavia, my editor at Crown/Random House, for making this book better than the manuscript he saw originally; Roberta Silman for her valuable insights and support. Lastly, and with great gratitude, my wife, Phyllis, my first and last reader and the reason I'm a writer.

Turn the page for a preview of *Sinner's Ball,*
Ira Berkowitz's next novel featuring Jackson Steeg.

Her name was Angela. She was a tiny fifteen-year-old runaway with flyaway hair, a face that was all hollows dense with shadows, and minutes left to live.

She had been in the city just shy of two months. Her older sister Wanda had run a year earlier, leaving Angela alone in their father's house.

You've got to get out, Wanda had said. I know what it's like. Know what he's like. Ma won't admit it. Probably glad he don't mess with her. It ain't gonna stop, Angie. Quit being a fraidy cat. Come to New York and live with me. It's cool. The people. The scene. All cool. There's work. I'll hook you up. Pays more money than you ever seen.

But Angela was a fraidy cat and stayed, kidding herself into believing it would stop.

Until the last time. He'd made her do things. Hurt her.

While he slept, Angela had crept into the garage, lifted all the cash from his secret hiding place, and headed for the Greyhound bus station in Davenport. Twenty-two stops and a little more than a day later she pulled into the Port Authority bus depot. Wanda met her and took her back to an apartment she shared with three other girls and a man they called Daddy. He told Angela she was part of the family now, and in his family everyone worked. Then he told her what work meant.

Angela ran. Again.

Until the streets caught her.

Now it was Christmas Eve. The temperature had dipped into the low teens and the wind blew the snow sideways. The sidewalk Santas were long gone, the carolers had packed it in, and all across the city, families, all warm and cozy, tossed the last piece of tinsel on the tree and settled in for the night.

In Hell's Kitchen, Angela and two brain-fried junkies she had met outside a warehouse hatched their own plan to celebrate the Savior's birth.

The guys—one with rat eyes and the other with sores on his face—had dug deep into their pockets and come up with enough for a dime bag of rock and the best bottle of wine three dollars could buy. Even though the thought of it made her feel as if spiders were crawling all over her skin, Angela chipped in her body for a couple of hits and a few hours of warmth. Then they jimmied a window and climbed into the warehouse.

Christmas Eve was for families, and it had been a long time since Angela had seen her sister. The zombies were all for it. Rat Eyes handed her a cell phone he had boosted a few days earlier. Wanda didn't answer, but Angela left the address.

And then it was party time.

Surrounded by stacks of cartons stuffed with counterfeit designer goods, they made short work of the rock and polished off the bottle with lying stories of Christmas Eves past. Now with eyes closed and heads propped against the cartons, they slept and dreamed Thunderbird dreams.

They never heard the whisper of flame smoldering deep within the walls or the frantic rustling of rats scurrying to the safety of the river. Never smelled the acrid odor of smoke as the flames crept up toward the dead space right under the roof.

And even if they had, it would have been too late.

■

Wanda sat in a musty bar thick with smoke, nursing a two-buck draft in a dirty pint glass, listening to Angela's message and weighing her options. Outside the streets were empty, shrouded in the muted glow of light filtered through giant flakes of whipping snow. She wasn't even close to making her three-hundred-dollar nut, and didn't have a prayer. But there was one thing she knew for a certainty, Daddy had to get paid. Didn't want to hear shit about blizzards or Christmas or any other stuff. You live in Daddy's house, you pay the rent. Every day. No ifs, ands, or buts.

Wanda reached into her bra and pulled out a thin wad of bills, adding them up one more time, thinking maybe she had made a mistake. Nope. Three twenties and a ten.

Fuck it! she thought, downing the beer and dropping her cigarette into the thin soup at the bottom of the glass. *If I'm gonna get a beating, it's gonna be for a good reason.* Besides, the warehouse wasn't too far away.

The flames were streaming through the windows on the lower floors when Wanda came up the street. Splashes of glass glittered like diamonds in the snow. She stood stock-still, her body unwilling to move. A man, standing across the street with his face framed in firelight, turned to look at her. The expression on his face made her guts shrivel, and she looked away. When she looked back, he was gone.

At the distant whine of sirens Wanda glanced back at the building and swiped a sleeve across her eyes.

There was nothing to be done.

The Red Devil had begun to feed.

I need you to meet me at Feeney's. Noon tomorrow. It's important.

My brother, Dave, had finally made an appearance.

It had been a Job-like year for my brother. He had always been pretty good at dodging whatever it was that outrageous fortune threw at him. But in a short few months he had hit the cosmic trifecta. A rival mobster's bomb blew off his left hand. His son, Anthony, blew off Dartmouth for a spot in the family business. Soon after, his wife, Franny, blew up their marriage. Three stunning body blows he never saw coming, and that discomfiting knowledge had turned him into a recluse.

It had been a long time since I'd heard from him. Then his message showed up on my answering machine.

It got my attention. Words like "need" had never been part of Dave's vocabulary.

A couple of hours before my meeting with Dave I awoke to a day that brought new meaning to the word "bleak." Sometime during the night, the boiler in my apartment house had finally gone belly-up, and my three rooms were as comfy as a meat locker. Outside, the banked mounds of the most recent snowstorm were stained black with soot. A stiff west wind drove a blanket of clouds the color of sewage over the city, promising more of the same.

When I arrived at Feeney's, a young, wiry-looking guy with shoulder-length blond hair stood out front smoking a cigarette and eyeing me with a psycho piranha grin. A Closed sign hung on the front door. The usual deal when my brother wanted complete privacy.

I reached for the doorknob and Ponytail sidled up real close.

"Can't you read, rummy?" he said. "The sign says you're gonna have to find another slop chute to drink your breakfast in."

This had all the makings of an adventure.

The snakes in my head awakened from their slumber and began to uncoil. It had been a while since they had graced me with their presence. Truth be told, I'd missed them, especially at times like this.

"And you are?" I said.

He placed the flat of his hand on my chest, his grin toying and eyes glistening with razor wire.

"Me? I'm the guy who tells you where you can or can't go."

Maybe it was the stupid grin, or the hand on my chest, or that the boiler in my apartment building had committed suicide. Nah, it was the "rummy" crack.

My left hand shot out and grabbed his hair, tugging his head toward me. The move kind of shortened the distance between my right hand and a spot just above the bridge of his nose. He went down as if he had been hit with a cattle prod.

I reached down and dragged him into Feeney's, leaving his body just inside the door.

Nick D'Amico, the proprietor, and one of Dave's deceptively jolly killers, was deep in conversation at the bar with Kenny Apple, another of Dave's gunmen. They both stared at me.

"Who's the new guy?" I said.

Nick looked over at Ponytail. "What the hell happened?"

"Your new doorman has an attitude problem."

"*Fuck!*" Nick said. "He ain't one of mine. Name's Tommy Cisco. He's with Anthony's crew."

"Anthony has a crew? You've got to be kidding."

"He thinks he does. What can I tell you?" He reached down, grabbed a handful of Cisco's hair and dragged him back outside. "Be right back, I gotta take the garbage out."

"Nice work," Kenny said.

"He pissed me off. So what's so important that I had to come out on a day like this?"

"You got anything better to do?"

"Actually, no."

Ever since the NYPD and I parted company, my plate has been pretty much half empty. Sometimes more. There's not much call for an ex–Homicide detective with one lung and a disability pension. Every now and then something comes along and, if it interests me, I handle it. The pay is usually crap, but I don't need much. The rest of the time I spend trying to figure out what to do with the rest of my life. At least, that's what I tell people. The truth is, I did figure it out, and I just didn't like the answer.

"How about a heads-up about what I'm walking into here?" I said.

Nick jerked his thumb toward the back of the room. "Dave'll tell you."

"He has *another* problem?"

"You might say. You better get over there, his blood's really up."

Nick had done a nice job putting Feeney's back together after the bomb that took Dave's hand had gutted the joint. The mahogany bar, the Wurlitzer, the tin ceiling with a fleur-de-lis hammered into every panel, everything looked as good as new. The same couldn't be said for my brother.

Feeney's was where Dave did business, and as usual, he was dressed for it. Navy blue pinstriped suit. Crisp white shirt. Soft gray tie. But that's where the resemblance to the *old* Dave ended. His eyes were listless recesses set in a face that had lost its certainty. The stump of his left hand was encased in a sheath of black leather, which he rubbed furiously against the pebbled remainder of a port wine stain on his cheek, an end-lessly humiliating blotch of congenital graffiti that even laser surgery couldn't completely erase.

When Dave rubbed his cheek, bad things were in the offing.

He and his son, Anthony, sat in a back booth across from a heavyset, cherubic-looking guy who appeared to be doing all the talking, punctuating each sentence with a twitch of his brush mustache.

After the bombing, in some truly convoluted act of loyalty, Anthony decided he wanted in. And in some truly screwed-up act of parenting, Dave agreed. It won't last, he had said. The kid's too soft for the life. Doesn't have the stomach for it. He'll be back in Hanover carving ice sculptures at the Winter Festival in under a month.

That made my brother oh-for-four in the prediction department.

Now Anthony, the avid apprentice, sat by the master's side, soaking in the ins and outs of organized crime. He flashed me a cold smile he had probably spent weeks rehearsing in front of a mirror.

I ignored him.

"You really tuned that guy up," Dave said. "What happened?"

"I guess you forgot to leave my name on the guest list," I said. "So, how're you doing?"

His lips twisted into a bitter smile. "Living the dream." His voice was a scrape of sandpaper, and so low I had to lean in to hear it.

Anthony giggled as if it were the funniest thing he'd ever heard.

The sight of Anthony working hard on becoming his father's Mini-Me got *my* blood up. I threw him a look, and the stupid giggle froze in his throat.

"What are you so pissy about?" Dave said.

I glanced at Anthony and back to Dave. "If you don't know, I'm sorry for you."

My brother waved his hand dismissively. "Don't worry about it," he said. He looked at his watch. "You're late."

"Screw you! Last time I checked, I'm not on your payroll."

"That may be about to change."

That got the attention of the snakes in my head.

"What's that supposed to mean?"

"How's Allie?"

"Fine. As soon as I finish here I'm meeting her and DeeDee for lunch."

Allie Lebow was the current and future love of my life. And DeeDee Santos was my best pal, a friendship forged on filling in the empty spaces in each other's lives.

"Allie's a keeper. And DeeDee," he said, smiling now, "that kid has some mouth on her. Always liked her."

"She'll be thrilled to hear it. Now, can we get back to that 'payroll' thing again?"

Dave jutted his chin toward the cherub. "This is Sal Lomascio. Sal, this is my brother, Jake." We shook hands. Dave looked back to me. "Sal's a friend," he said. "Sit."

Sal moved his briefcase from the seat and set it on the table. I squeezed in next to him.

"Sal's an investigator for Pytho Insurance Group," Dave said. "We go way back."

Anthony, the apt pupil, smiled a crooked smile. The kid was trying too hard.

"Anyway," Dave continued, "we're talking about that fire I had over at my warehouse."

He said it dismissively, as if it were a simple kitchen flare-up that took out a couple of oven mitts, rather than a three-alarmer that turned three squatters into stains on the floor and cost two firefighters their lives.

"What about it?" I said.

"Pytho is refusing to pay."

I turned to Sal, not even bothering to keep the anger out of my voice. "You and Dave go way back. Fix it."

Anthony looked at me as if I were the dumbest guy in the room. "It's not that simple," he said.

Dave beat me to it. "Shut the fuck up, Anthony," he said.

My nephew's gaze wobbled and his cheeks went red. In a

heartbeat Anthony had gone from being the favored son to a minion, and was having a hard time keeping it together. Welcome to your new life, kid, I thought, not without sadness.

"Not this time," Sal said. "It was arson."

"And you know that how?" I said.

"It's my job. Let me give you the picture, here. Arson ain't like it is in the movies. You know, where the handsome lead detective spots this mook standing on the fringe of the crowd with his eyes rolling around in his head like he's about to come and sporting a hard-on you could cut diamonds with, and hauls his ass in to the station house and hammers him until he confesses."

"I love movies like that. Always made me feel good about my career choice."

"Trouble is, without proof of an accelerant, you got jack."

"And you found no accelerant."

His mustache twitched. "Bingo! So then you look for a shitload of circumstantial evidence and hope that it points somewhere."

"And you have that."

"Yeah. And it all starts with the real estate market."

"Hell of a circumstance."

"Right now, you bet your ass it is. Ever since the subprime mortgage bubble blew up, real estate prices dropped off the cliff. Properties like Dave's that were on the market at gonzo inflated values suddenly slid twenty, thirty percent or more and went begging even at the discount. So, what's an owner to do?"

"Like they used to say when there was a garment industry in this city, 'If you can't make a flood, make a fire,' " I said.

"Exactly. And Pytho has had a bunch of them lately. Sloppy, amateurish jobs. Fucker hires a couple of lame-ass torches, and they go at it with a couple of containers of gasoline."

"Tough to find good help these days."

"Tell me about it," Sal agreed.

"So, if there wasn't an accelerant at Dave's warehouse, what was it?"

"Two points of origin." Sal's eyes twinkled, and his mustache gave a self-congratulatory twitch. "That was the first clue. It took a lot of looking, but I could tell from the charring. The doer bored small holes in the lath and plaster walls, stuffed them with news-papers, and lit it up. Basically, you had a classic fire tetrahedron: fuel, oxygen, heat, and what eventually became—as we say in the arson game—an uninhibited chemical reaction."

"I don't get it. Lath is metal, and plaster doesn't burn."

"That's now. Unfortunately for the stiffs, the warehouse was built around 1900. Back then the lath was wood, and so are the floors."

"Not a happy circumstance."

"You might say. Everything was going on real slow inside the walls. But when the Red Devil hit the flooring and made it to the crates full of all that Chinese import shit, it just had more to eat. It took a couple of hundred firefighters with their snot turned to icicles to put it out. It was one hairy job."

"What about the sprinklers?"

"Fucked. We figure before the party got started the party-goers tried to rip out some piping, sell it, and maybe do some Christmas shopping. With brass going for close to two bucks a pound, they could score enough shit to last a few days. But all the poor bastards managed to do was break the pipe that fed the sprinkler."

"Bad things tend to happen to the least of us. The way of the world. But how does this lead back to Dave?"

"In and of itself, it doesn't," Sal said.

I turned to my brother. "I don't see the problem, Dave. Pytho refuses to pay, tough shit. A cost of doing business. All you're out is some money."

"There's more," Dave said.

"Why is it there's always more?"

Sal closed his briefcase and locked it. "We found six bodies in the basement. In coffins. Looked like a funeral parlor showroom, all neat and lined up a few feet from each other."

"This is a new one," I said.

"For me too. I call them coffins, but they were really sealed metal boxes with air holes punched in the side. Twelve of them. But only six contained bodies. The others were empty. And here's the thing. When we pried them open, there was a full-length mirror under each lid. And as an added attraction, we found one of those key-ring flashlights in each of the boxes. All the comforts of home."

"Sweet Jesus! They watched themselves die?"

"Fucked up, huh? But just when you think it can't get better, it does."

"I can hardly wait."

"According to the medical examiner, at least four of the guys were alive when the fire took them. Talked to each other too. And maybe to the guy who put them there."

"What do you mean, 'talked to each other'?"

"Each box had one of those walkie-talkies. Talk about your basic horror show."

"I don't get it," I said.

"Neither do I," Dave said. "I put the warehouse on the market six months ago, locked it up, and walked away. No one had access."

"What about the counterfeit stuff?"

"Ever since the latest Fed crackdown, I got out of the business. Left it to the Chinatown gangs. Too much risk, not enough reward. Whatever Nick couldn't move on the street, I left sitting there, growing mold."

"And you have no idea where the bodies came from?"

"Not a clue."

"Let's put it this way," Sal said. "They were so fucked up, we're down to checking dental records and waiting on a toxicology report."

"Look, Jake," Dave said, using the nickname he tagged me with when we were kids. "We know how this is going to go down. The DA is all about expedience. He looks at my line of work, sees the stiffs, puts two and two together, and comes up with the brilliant deduction that I iced those guys. I take the fall, another case cleared, crime wave over. Am I wrong?"

Dave wasn't wrong. If anything, he didn't go far enough. This was an election year, and politics trumped everything. The DA had been in office since there were trolley cars and had reached the limit of his wear-out factor. But he wasn't quite ready for a drool cup and lap robe. There was one last hurrah on his to-do list before going gently into that good night. A high-profile case could be just the ticket. And Dave, the reigning Hell's Kitchen Kingpin of Crime, fit the bill very nicely.

"You pretty much summed it up," I said.

"My lawyer tells me that an indictment is about to come down."

"Not good."

"Not good at all. What's worse is that my life has turned into a line from a telemarketing commercial."

"What do you mean?"

" '*But wait, there's more!*' Yeah, something's going on. A pattern, like. And the fire is just a piece of it. Someone's moving into the Kitchen. Muscling bookies, ripping off poker games, and playing general fuckaround. They haven't hit any of my operations yet, but I get the feeling it's right around the corner."

"What do your guys say?"

"So far? Nothing. Nobody's got a line on these guys. Could be the guineas, the spics, the Russians, or some other flavor of asshole thinking about trying me on for size. Since the, uh, incident"—he stroked his cheek with the stump of his hand—"the jokers probably think I'm, you know, vulnerable. But they don't know who they're fucking with, do they?"

"I don't want to know about it."

He smiled a crooked smile. "Whatever. But I'll tell you this. When I find them, I'm going to rip out their eyes and use 'em for marbles."

Nothing ever changes.

"Have you heard from Franny?" I said.

His face went cold.

"Like I said, I need *you*, Jake. Just you and me together. Just like old times."

Just like old times.